THE
GIRLS AT
17 SWANN STREET

Center Point
Large Print

**This Large Print Book carries the
Seal of Approval of N.A.V.H.**

THE
GIRLS AT
17 SWANN
STREET

YARA ZGHEIB

CENTER POINT LARGE PRINT
THORNDIKE, MAINE

This Center Point Large Print edition
is published in the year 2019 by arrangement with
St. Martin's Press.

The text of this Large Print edition is unabridged.
In other aspects, this book may vary
from the original edition.
Printed in the United States of America
on permanent paper.
Set in 16-point Times New Roman type.

ISBN: 978-1-64358-114-9

Library of Congress Cataloging-in-Publication Data

Names: Zgheib, Yara, author.
Title: The girls at 17 Swann Street / Yara Zgheib.
Description: Center Point Large Print edition. | Thorndike, Maine :
    Center Point Large Print, 2019.
Identifiers: LCCN 2018059422 | ISBN 9781643581149 (hardcover :
    alk. paper)
Subjects: LCSH: Psychological fiction. | Large type books.
Classification: LCC PS3626.G44 G57 2019b | DDC 813.6—dc23
LC record available at https://lccn.loc.gov/2018059422

To you, who, in these pages,
found your reading glasses, sweatshirt,
earrings, favorite book or flavor of ice cream,
freckles, perfume, signature crêpe recipe,
nose twitch, stutter, or missing sock

I

I call it the Van Gogh room. Just a different color scheme. Hazy peach blanket, hazy peach walls. Pastel-green carpet on a cherrywood floor. White blinds and shutters, the window and closet creak. Everything looks pale and tired, a little like me.

I look around and think, *This is where it starts.* In Bedroom 5, on the east side of a pink house at 17 Swann Street. As good, as bad a setting as any, I suppose, for a story like this. Plain and mildly inviting, dubiously clean. At least there is a window; I can see the driveway, the edge of the street, bits of garden and sky.

Four hangers, four towels, four shelves. I have not packed much, I do not need more. I have, however, packed my makeup kit, a red one my mother used to own. Not that I need it; I will not be going anywhere for a long time. No work shift to check into on Monday morning, no plans for the weekend. But I will look nice, I have to. I set the kit on the white shelf and dab blush on my cheeks.

Deodorant, coconut lotion. My apple and jasmine perfume. A spritz behind each ear, two more. I will not smell like a hospital bed.

7

Four magnets on a whiteboard. Oh, I will need much more. For the time being, I spread my thick stack of photographs in a rainbow on the floor. I contemplate all the faces I have loved in my life and put up my favorite four.

My mother and father. *Maman et Papa*, on the faded day they eloped. She in her borrowed white dress and white shoes, he in his father's suit.

A picture of Sophie, Camil, and me on a picnic by a stream. It must have been autumn; the sky above us was cloudy. Camil must have been five or six; Leopold in his lap was still a puppy.

Matthias, gorgeous Matthias squinting at the sun and my lens. The first picture I took of him, that first morning in Paris. A quietly happy day.

Last, Matthias and me, mouths covered in chocolate, hands holding messy half-eaten crêpes. Our official wedding photo, posed for proudly outside the Métro three years ago.

The kaleidoscope goes by the bed, the slippers and a box underneath. Blinds up, night-light on.

I have moved into Bedroom 5, 17 Swann Street.

My name is Anna. I am a dancer, a constant daydreamer. I like sparkling wine in the late afternoon, ripe and juicy strawberries in June. Quiet mornings make me happy, dusk makes me blue. Like Whistler, I like gray and foggy cities. I see purple in gray and foggy days. I believe in the rich taste of real vanilla ice cream, melting stickily from a cone. I believe in love. I am madly in love, I am madly loved.

I have books to read, places to see, babies to make, birthday cakes to taste. I even have unused birthday wishes to spare.

So what am I doing here?

I am twenty-six years old. My body feels sixty-two. So does my brain. Both are tired, irritable, in pain. My hair was once wild-lion thick, morning blond. It is now a nondescript, mousy beige that falls in wisps around my face and out in my hands. My eyes, green like my mother's, are sunk so deep in their sockets that no makeup will fill the craters. I do have lovely eyelashes. I always liked those. They curl up at the edges like those of a doll I used to own.

My collarbones, ribs, kneecaps, and streamer-like thin blue veins peek through paper-thin skin. My skin, largest organ of my body and its first line of defense, has been more decorative than functional lately. In fact, not even that; it is cracked and taut, constantly bruised and cold. Today it smells of baby oil. For the occasion, I used lavender.

I have a flat stomach. I once had lips and breasts, but those shrank months ago. Along with my thighs, my liver, my behind. I lost my sense of humor too.

I do not laugh very often anymore. Very little is funny. When I do, it sounds different. So does my voice on the telephone. Apparently. Not that I can tell the difference: I do not have many people to call.

I realize that my phone is not with me, then remember; they took it away. I am allowed to have it until 10:00 A.M. and after dinner in the evenings. One of the many house rules I will have to learn while I am living here, however long that will be. How long will that be? I turn away from the thought . . .

. . . and hit a tidal wave of panic. I do not recognize the girl, or the reality I just described.

2

Clinical Intake and Assessment Form

Friday—May 20, 2016
Patient Identification Information
Name: Anna M. Roux, maiden name Aubry
Date of birth: November 13, 1989
Place of birth: Paris, France
Sex: Female
Age: 26

Emergency Contact Information
Name: Matthias Roux
Relationship: Spouse

General Background
Occupation:
I tell people I am a dancer. I have not danced in years, though. I work as a cashier in a supermarket, but my real occupation is anorexia.
Marital Status: Married.
Children: None.
Yet. Hopefully, maybe, after this is all over?
I skip Ethnic Background, Family and Social History, Education, and Hobbies.

Physical Health

I feel fine, thank you.

Allergies: **None.**

Last menstrual cycle: **Unknown.**

I cannot remember.

Birth control? Contraceptive medication?

What for? And what for?

Weight and height: *None of your business.*

Patient's weight: **88 lbs.**

Patient's height: **5' 4"**

BMI: **15.1**

So I am a little underweight. So what?

Daily Habits

Tobacco:

No. *I do not like the smell.*

Alcohol:

A glass of wine, once a week on a Friday night.

Recreational drugs:

No.

Caffeine:

How else do you think I function on only three hours of sleep?

Number of meals eaten on a normal week-day:

Define the words "normal" and "meal." I keep a few apples in my bag in case I get too hungry.

Number of meals eaten on a normal weekend day:

Why would that be different? Well, I do some-

12

times make popcorn in the microwave. Single serving. Nonfat.

Regular exercise routine: **Yes.**

Naturally.

Frequency: **Every day.**

Please describe:

I run, build strength, and stretch for two hours, every morning before 7:00 A.M.

What do you do to manage stress?

I run, build strength, and stretch for two hours every morning before 7:00 A.M.

Mental Health

Basic problem or concern: **Difficulty eating certain foods.**

Difficulty eating, period. Loss of interest in food, loss of interest in general.

Significant changes or stressors in recent history: **None**

that I have any interest in disclosing here.

Previous mental health diagnoses: **None.**

I said I feel fine.

Feelings of sadness?

Check.

Hopelessness?

Check.

Anxiety?

Check check.

Please check any symptoms experienced in the past month:

Restricted food intake.
Check.
Compulsion to exercise.
Check.
Avoidance of certain foods.
Check.
Laxative abuse.
Check.
Binge.
Check. *A whole box of blackberries last week.*
Self-induced vomiting.
Only with guilt. See above on blackberries.
Concerns about weight, body image, feeling fat.
Check. Check. Check.
Total weight lost over the past year:
Pass.
Lowest weight ever reached:
Pass again.
These questions are inappropriate.
Diagnosis
Anorexia nervosa. Restricting type.

3

The bedroom, the whole flat in fact, was an industrial cube. The sort of unit prized by cost-cutting developers and lower-income tenants. High ceiling and concrete walls left provocatively naked, lined with steel pipes. More loft than apartment unit, more studio really.

Light flowed in buckets through the one window that covered the only external wall. She walked up to it and looked down onto a little patch of green, across onto the next building, up onto the third floor and window parallel to theirs. The blinds were drawn. Did neighbours know their neighbours here? There was no "u" in the word "neighbors" here. She would have to remember that.

"Flat" was not the right word either, she reminded herself. Flats here were called apartments. She was in America now.

Apartment. America. She tried both words on for size, feeling them on her tongue as she rolled them around in her mouth. This apartment was bare but it was theirs, small but luxurious by Parisian standards.

In Paris they had been living in a cupboard of

a room, sharing a wall, bathroom, little stove and fridge with a philosophy major, a psychologist, their lovers, and a computer technician who was never there but made outstanding pesto when he was. Bohemian life did not scare her; she had always loved and led it happily. But this was not bohemian, or Paris. This was the American Midwest.

She had landed last night. Matthias had been waiting at the airport with a red rose. He had driven her here. Dinner, wine, sex, and this morning he had left for work . . .

. . . and had not said when he would return, Anna realized. She finished unpacking—apple and jasmine perfume, lotion, hairbrush, tooth-brush next to his. Books by the bed. She had forgotten her slippers. Done. Eleven o'clock.

One more look around. The walls were not too bare. She would cover them with photographs of home. She would also buy groceries, candles, and some more wine. Would Matthias be home for lunch?

Surely not. But she would make sure dinner was ready when he did. They would have a feast, then go out to explore this new city. Till then . . .

She hummed notes at random and walked toward the fridge. A quarter of the pizza Matthias had ordered the night before remained. He had left the crusts on the side; he knew Anna liked them. There was also a piece of cheese, some yogurt, a few fruits. She took the yogurt and some strawberries.

Where would she eat them, though? They had no furniture yet beyond the coffee table and the bed. Coffee table then. She would just sit on the floor.

She boiled water and stirred in instant coffee. One sip. Disaster. Enough. That was not coffee. She poured it into the sink and decided she would have tea.

They did not have tea. Eleven oh five. The yogurt was the fruity kind, with syrup. She put it back in the fridge and ate the strawberries. Eleven oh six. It would soon be time for lunch anyway. She reached for the phone, then put it down; it was late afternoon in Paris and everyone was surely busy now.

Perhaps she would go for a run before lunch. Matthias just might be back then.

He was not. She showered and slowly went through her lotion routine, dried her hair, put on a blue dress, reached for a red makeup kit: face cream, mascara, peach blush. Pink lipstick applied. Twelve twenty-eight.

Fridge. Pizza, crust, cheese, yogurt, and fruit. She should buy groceries for the evening. She could make crêpes and a salad. Cheese and mushrooms. They would have the fruit for dessert.

Twelve twenty-nine. She would go before lunch.

One thirty in the afternoon and she finally had everything she needed. The store she had spotted on her run had not been as close as she had thought. Her voice had croaked mildly at the cash register; she was using it for the first time that day. A while later, the eggs, milk, flour, ricotta, and lettuce, mushrooms, tomatoes were in the fridge. Done.

Concrete walls. She took the phone and put it down. Opened and closed the fridge. She took two of Matthias's leftover crusts, ripped them into little bits, and slowly chewed the first, looking out the large window, exhaling the anxiety away.

Nine full minutes later it was done. She hated eating alone. At 1:41 she took the blue dress off and hung it neatly with the rest of her clothes. All she owned had moved from one suitcase to twenty hangers and a shelf in cube 315 of many more in the building on 45 Furstenberg Street. She climbed back into bed.

Matthias would be back soon anyway and then she would make the crêpes.

4

I do not suffer from anorexia, I have anorexia. The two states are not the same. I know my anorexia, I understand it better than the world around me.

The world around me is obese, half of it. The other half is emaciated. Values are hollow, but meals are dense with high fructose corn syrup. Standards come in doubles, so do portions. The world is overcrowded but lonely. My anorexia keeps me company, comforts me. I can control it, so I choose it.

The *Diagnostic and Statistical Manual of Mental Disorders* (Fifth Edition) defines anorexia nervosa as a brain disease, a mental disorder with severe metabolic effects on the entire body. Characteristics:

1. *Restriction of food, self-induced starvation with the purpose of losing weight.*
2. *An intense fear of gaining weight or becoming fat.*
3. *A distorted perception of body weight or shape with a strong influence on mental well-being,*

as well as
a lack of awareness of the severity of the condition.

I run for eighty minutes each day, build strength for another twenty, keep my caloric intake below eight hundred calories, a thousand when I binge. I weigh myself every morning and cry at the number on the scale. I cry in front of mirrors too: I see fat everywhere.

Everyone around me thinks I have a problem. Everyone around me is scared. I do not have a problem. I just have to lose a little bit of weight. I am scared too, but not of gaining weight. I am terrified of life. Of a sad and unfair world. I do not suffer from a sick brain. I suffer from a sick heart.

Cardiac arrhythmia. Irregular heartbeat. Like falling in love, or a heart attack.

Cardiomyopathy. Loss of heart muscle mass. Yes, but only the excess.

I do not need dispensable tissue, dispensable fat or organs. But my body is greedy; it wants more potassium, sodium, magnesium. Energy.

My body does not know what it needs. I make that decision for it. In protest, my heart pumps less blood. *Bradycardia.* Slow heartbeat. My blood pressure drops.

The rest of my body follows suit, falling quietly, like rain, like snow. My ovaries, my liver, my kidneys go next. Then my brain goes to sleep.

5

Anna? Should I pause the movie? You are missing the good parts.

Anna?

Anna, are you all right in there? Open the door please.

Anna, open the door! Anna!

6

Matthias found me on the floor, legs like cotton, mouth numb. I could feel the bathroom tiles, freezing, painful against my back, but I was also falling through them. I could not grasp the wisps of words I needed to tell him that I was fine. I could not grasp his shirt; my hands were clumsy. My thoughts were clumsy too.

I could not move my hands, I could not move. Matthias carried me from the bathroom into the bedroom.

For a few minutes neither of us said anything. The movie was on pause too. I wanted to press Play, end the ugly intermission. Matthias had other plans.

We need to talk, Anna.
What about?
What happened in there?
I fell in the bathroom, Matthias,
I sliced.
I am fine now. I just stood up too fast.

Muscles tense, defenses up, circling the ring. He could feel the edge in my voice. He circled too, carefully.

23

What about yesterday, during your shift? And last week, when you hurt your shoulder?

I was tired! I slipped!

We need to talk, Anna.

We are talking!

We need to stop lying then.

Matthias was a few years older than I was, thirty-one in a couple of months. He looked older just then. Our voices had been rising, but he said that last sentence very quietly.

Another lull while he chose his words. I did not, would not, help him.

I think you need treatment. I've been a coward. I should have spoken a long time ago. I just kept convincing myself you were fine—

I told you: I am fine!

My claws were out, a cat trapped in a corner.

I know things have been difficult since Christmas, but I have this under control! I've been eating normally—

You've lost so much weight—

How would you know, Matthias? You're never here!

I had gone on the offensive, he had left me no choice. My back was to the wall and I needed air. But the shriller I got, the calmer he did.

You're right. I am not. I'm sorry.

I do not need you to be sorry, or worry about me! I can take care of myself! I told you: I am fine—

And I believed you, because I wanted to.
I cannot anymore, Anna.

I do not remember much of the three years that led up to that moment. Just that they felt long and cold, and I felt underwater in them. The two days that followed, however, flashed by to Matthias and me getting in the car and driving up an empty Highway 44 to an address on Swann Street. It took us just under forty-five minutes. Really, it took us much longer; three years and twenty-two pounds to reach that Intake and Assessment appointment.

7

It was Thursday night and freezing, but the Christmas displays were worth it, Anna decided as she wrapped her plush white scarf tighter around her neck. Digging her gloved hands deeper into her coat, she walked down the Grands Boulevards, window to window, drummer boys and nutcrackers, twinkling lights and whimsical trains.

She bumped into him, or he into her. Either way,

Oh, je suis désolée!

But he smiled. She smiled. What a coincidence, he was also walking that way. They walked together, to the end of the display. Then they kept walking and talking.

They walked through ample sidewalk and conversation. Then it was cold, so they went inside. They had two glasses of Bordeaux, each. They shared a basket of fries.

His name was Matthias and he said she was beautiful. They kissed. Then,

Shall we get some ice cream?

Ice cream? It was freezing! Was he mad?

It cannot make us any colder.

Good point.
On one condition, though:
I want it in a cone.
Un cornet pour mademoiselle!
She giggled and they bundled up and linked arms and walked out into the cold again.

They walked across the bridge, past the colorful cafés where tourists were gladly being swindled. Left onto a side street, all the way down, to a well-hidden little kiosk.

The queue outside it was a good sign, and that there were no tourists in it. He had two scoops: chocolate and something pink. She had her vanilla and her cone. They ate as they walked and shivered and stopped to kiss stickily.

Would you like to have dinner with me tomorrow night?

It was the easiest yes in history.

No, actually, it was not. That came later, one year later in the same place.

Lips and fingers sticky, he asked:

Would you like to marry me?

They were married in the first week of January, the coldest wedding in history.

They had croissants from the boulangerie downstairs for breakfast. She made coffee on the little stove. They froze in the snow, he in his only suit, she in the creamy white dress she had bought. They stepped out of the mairie *at noon holding hands, kissing, laughing at the words "husband" and "wife," and just before ducking into the Métro, they had gooey crêpes for their wedding lunch.*

8

There must have been signs that we were taking a detour from the happily-ever-after road.

I got an offer today,

Matthias said one afternoon.

An offer? For what?

I sipped my tea. Matthias's serious face had Nutella on it. I smiled.

A job offer. In the States!

More tea. His excited face. His *I want this* face. The States. Well . . .

Why not? Perhaps the timing was perfect. I would be removing my cast in a few weeks and needed a fresh start. My spot in the Opéra's corps de ballet—left stage, second swan from the wings—had been promptly and easily filled after the accident. The show had had to go on. No hard feelings.

I could dance in the States, had never been to the States.

Where is the offer?

Saint Louis,

like the name of the picturesque island where we had kissed on our first date. I imagined quaint little cafés and shops lining quaint little streets. *Saint Louis.* Perhaps it was a sign. Would they have good ice cream?

Well, I will not be eating ice cream, I said sternly to myself. I had not danced or run in months. I had to get back in shape. Till I was, I would diet, and follow Matthias, apparently, why not, to the States. I watched him lick Nutella off his fingers. I kissed what remained on his chin.

He left Paris first with the first of our suitcases. I packed the rest of our lives in the second. We had one-way tickets and a plan and each other. There was no way we could get lost.

There must have been signs, but we were distracted by the roller coaster of the adventure. Paperwork, looking for a couch for the apartment, ties and shirts for Matthias.

Looking for a ballet company I could join. It was small but we eventually found it.

And were told that their corps de ballet was full, *but thank you for applying.*

It's all right,
said Matthias.
We will keep looking.
It's all right,
I echoed. We did. There must have been signs, but we missed them, too busy, him working, me trying to.

I spent months getting myself back in shape and searching for other opportunities. The pickings were slim, or my bar was too high, or Saint Louis was not a ballet kind of town. I could not find another dance company, or the quaint cafés on quaint little streets.

I found other jobs and went to job interviews, but I was not qualified for those. I was a dancer applying to be a store manager, a bank teller. *What experience do you have?*

There were signs: foods I slowly stopped eating, dresses I slowly stopped putting on. They got too loose, and I have nowhere to wear them anyway.

Waiting for Matthias to come home from work so I would not have to eat alone. When he did:

Any luck today, Anna?

He eventually stopped asking.

Eventually, I also stopped searching. And dairy, and answering my phone. And wearing makeup, but at least I was not fat anymore.

Other signs: long days I made shorter with longer runs, longer showers, longer naps. Photos of us that looked less and less like me. But somehow, we did not see.

There was nothing mysterious about the road we took to 17 Swann Street. Hundreds of girls have taken it before me to this suburban house painted peach pink. With some variation: some drive or fly in, from out of town, out of country, out of state. The lucky ones are driven by family or friends. The unlucky, ambulances. Some come by way of restriction, pills, laxatives, and exercise. Some from the other direction by bingeing, purging comfort food. Some run in, chasing love and acceptance, some fleeing depression, anxiety. Puddles of murky emotions in potholes of boredom, loneliness, guilt.

There were signs. There are always signs for those who know to look for them. They just never flash in red neon, warning, Danger: Risk of Death.

They begin a few miles from the Swann Street exit:

No thank you, I am not hungry.

I do not like chocolate, or cheese. I am allergic to gluten, nuts, and dairy. And I do not eat meat.

I already had dinner. I am going for a run. No, do not wait up for me.

Then bones stick out. Hair and nails fall out. Everything hurts and it is cold. Past the hundred-pound mark. Ninety-five pounds. Ninety-three. Ninety-one, eighty-nine.

Eighty-eight.

9

It happened so fast. On Friday I was shivering in a flower-print robe while from every angle sterile blue gloves poked and prodded at me. My heart was listened to. Ears, eyes, throat observed. My reflexes and pulse were recorded. Bone density scan, blood and urine analyses, ECG, height and weight.

Diagnosis: Anorexia nervosa.

Recommended level of care: Residential treatment, effective Monday morning. 9:00 A.M.

Monday morning, the twenty-third of May. We were there right on time, Matthias and I and the silence and my blue suitcase with the red bow. We sat in the driveway for a minute, or ten.

Please say something, Anna.

Beat.

There is nothing to say.

Come on, Anna! We can't just stay here like this, in the car.

Would you like me to get out?

That is not what I meant!

Silence again. His hand idle on the gearbox. Mine stubbornly clenching my thigh. I did not know if he was looking at me; I was staring firmly ahead. I could not see, but I did not dare blink the blur away. If I did I knew the tears would come streaming down and I could not, would not, let them.

Nothing to say. What a petty, passive aggressive lie. But I was so angry I could not speak, and all of my anger was directed at Matthias; there was no one else around. I felt like a box of worn and frayed winter clothes that he was donating away.

His hand on the gearbox. He had not held mine, or held me at all, in fact, in a long time. It was only partly his fault; his hands make mine cold and his touch, even gentle, often hurts. Last night, in bed, I had shuddered when he had lifted the covers to slide under them. His weight had shifted the mattress, which had dug painfully into my hip. I had snapped at him and hugged myself against the cold air that had rushed in.

I had not spoken to him since then. Now, goodbyes in the car.

You do not need to come inside with me. I can wheel the suitcase in on my own.

I knew I was hurting him but could not help the spite coming out of my mouth. I could not bear the thought that he was leaving, that he was leaving me here.

Do you really think I'm going to drop you off and just leave?

Why not?

I answered spitefully.

Isn't that why we are here?

For him to hand me and this pesky problem over to someone else?

Matthias got testy:

And you think this is easy for me? Bringing you here?

But there was no space for empathy in my dangerously swollen chest. Suddenly, it exploded.

I would not know! You do not talk to me either! Or kiss me, or make love to me! You have not told me you loved me in weeks. You do not even look at me!

He looked at me then, stunned, and I already regretted what I had begun, but it was too late. I fired the rest of my anger and fear at him:

You got tired of dealing with me, feeding me! That's fine! Someone else will now and with me gone you can finally have your life back. You can open the window, have the whole bed to yourself, go to restaurants every night—

I don't want the bed to myself! I don't want the restaurants! I want you, Anna!

Then don't leave me here . . .

My voice and I broke down. No longer angry, I was begging. Crying and scared. *Please.*

Please, Matthias, let's go home,

I said in a whisper. *Please,*

even as he and I both knew we could not.

His voice was tired when he spoke:

37

We can't go home, Anna.

Low and heavy:

I didn't drive you here to get rid of you. I did because I can't lose you. I can't live without you. Do you understand, Anna? I can't lose you—

He stopped. His voice was shaky too.

My left hand moved involuntarily, imperceptibly toward the gearbox. His hand waited. I hesitated, then finally reached for it. He looked at me and I burst into tears and a flurry of words spilled out.

What if you cannot manage on your own? You do not know how to cook! What if you need to do laundry and forget how to set the machine?

And the real fears:

What if I stay in this place so long that you forget the way I smell? What if you forget me?

Then:

What if you meet someone else?

Impossible,

and he kissed me for a long time, for the first time in weeks.

We sat in the car, my hand on his. Now there really was nothing left to say. After a while, he helped me with my suitcase and we went inside together.

10

There is a knock at the door of the Van Gogh room. A head does not wait to pop in.

Good, I see you have unpacked. Time for orientation now.

Admission begins, sickeningly cold and impersonal. I am swept into a current of intake forms, vitals, inventory, insurance. Down to business as soon as finances are cleared. The white coats unfold: the primary care physician, the psychiatrist, a nurse. Then follow the suits: the psychologist, the nutritionist, and the first of a stream of look-alike staff members I would come to know only as Direct Care.

Meal plan, treatment plan, rules of the house. Session plan, towels and sheets, rules of the game.

I sign a form that states that I am here voluntarily. Then about twenty more: no drugs, no alcohol, no smoking on the premises, even when out on the porch. My legal rights, my patient rights, the conditions for any release of medical information to family.

Then a few more morbid ones I choose not to take seriously: That I will not burn myself, cut or harm myself or others. That I will hand all sharp objects to staff. That I will not kill myself.

I sign, deliberately offhandedly, one form after the next, trying not to understand what they mean: that this nightmare is real. But at the very last form, I freeze:

The document states that I will lose all my rights—to object, to refuse, to leave—if the institution or Matthias believe I am not of sound mind, or at risk.

Lose all my rights. Not of sound mind. Not burn, cut, or kill myself. No time: Direct Care snatches the last form out of my hands.

Now the schedule:

My days will begin at 5:30 A.M., in a blue flower-print robe she gives me.

You can wear it however you want,

the lady explains.

Flap at the back or front.

Flap at the back says hospital, I think. Flap at the front then, like a spa.

Once vitals and weights are taken,

she says,

you can change back into your clothes. You can also go back to sleep.

Like I could do that in a place like this, I snort. Like I could do that at all.

Breakfast is at eight, downstairs in community space, where I will have to stay all day. Within the premises, and well within view of the nurse's station and Direct Care. Midmorning and late-evening snacks are served there too; I should sign up for those each day. All other meals will be served in the house next door. Menus for those are planned on Thursday.

No outside food, no food outside those times. The cook plates and wraps every meal. I am to eat every dish set in front of me within a specific time: thirty minutes for breakfast and snacks, forty-five for lunch and dinner. Failure to complete the meal means drinking a nutritional supplement. Failing that is a refusal. Three refusals means a feeding tube, and she assures me I do not want one of those.

Forty-eight hours in and pending good behavior, you can go on the morning walk.

It will be led by a member of staff to ensure a leisurely pace. If it is raining, the walk will be postponed to the following day. No other exercise or time outdoors. I pray for a month of sunny days.

All the bathrooms are locked, and outside those, there are no mirrors on the walls. We must all ask for permission every time we have to go. Direct Care will then pull out her keys, their humiliating jingle announcing loud and clear to everyone else that I need to empty my bladder.

Some of the girls' bathroom use itself has to be monitored; they cannot go or flush alone. A precautionary rule against purging, cutting, or attempts at suicide. But I am not bulimic, and at least so far, have not expressed interest in self-harm. I am therefore graciously informed that I may use the bathroom alone. I will, however, have to report how much fluid I drink throughout the day. But that is only temporary and, if my kidneys behave, she says, that rule will be revoked in a week.

Whenever I am not eating I will be in session, individual or group. The therapist will see me three times a week, the nutritionist twice, the psychiatrist once. No phones or other electronics during programming hours; no distractions from eating and fixing the mess I have made in my body and brain.

Oh, and one more thing,
she says.
A note on terminology.
Certain words and phrases are inappropriate here. She calls them *triggering*. No talk of food or exercise, no mention of weight or calories. My disease is not to be mentioned by name; a vague *eating disorder* is fine. If I am sad and want to die, I should say I am *struggling*. If I want to run away, throw myself under a bus, then I am having *an urge*. If I feel fat or worthless or ugly, I have *body image issues*. These verbal gymnastics are to be applied at all times and to every sub-ject.

I should, she insists, always *communicate* my

thoughts and feelings freely. Staff is here to *validate* those and *redirect* my behaviors,

and by the end of treatment, you will be cured of ano—your eating disorder.

Direct Care wraps up orientation with a sympathetic, condescending smile. The professionally appropriate, if slightly distracted, smile of a time-clock employee. She has given this speech hundreds of times to hundreds of girls just like me. Her mind is already on other things. Mine remains frozen in place.

II

As soon as orientation ends, another staff member comes to me.

Ready to meet with your therapist?

The tone of the question gives me the impression that I am not really being asked.

Minutes later, I am sitting on a gray suede couch in a nice office, on the edge closest to the window. There is a magnolia tree outside.

The therapist walks in. First impressions: bright blond hair, the warm kind, fine gold earrings, a turquoise dress. An impeccable pedicure and soft peony perfume. Her face looks fresh, but a slight crease around her eyes belies children at home under five.

Hello. I'm Katherine. You must be Anna.

I nod and proceed immediately to tell her that I do not need this session. She seems like a lovely lady, and I do not want to waste her time. I suffer from no psychiatric illnesses, except anorexia, of course. I come from a loving family and have a husband I adore by whom I sleep every night.

No depression or trauma, at least none that I need or am inclined to share. No unhealed wounds from my past or skeletons in my closet

I need to address. I am just particular about what I eat, just a little underweight.

Thank you for your time. I'm fine.

She waits a few seconds, then repeats my speech to be sure she has understood.

So you're happy.

Yes.

You feel fine.

Yes.

You don't need therapy because you have no mental issues that need to be addressed.

Correct.

So when was the last time you ate?

I decide I hate therapy and proceed to draw butterflies with my finger on the couch.

All right,

she says,

what if we set anorexia aside for now? What if you tell me a bit about your childhood?

I glance at the clock on the wall.

You're stuck with me for a full hour,

she adds. I decide I might as well.

I had a happy childhood.

Full, as childhoods should be, of picnics in parks, make-believe tea parties, bedtime stories, poetry.

My parents were good, hardworking people who married out of love. I had two younger siblings: a sister and a brother. He . . .

Had?

46

No, I will not answer that. Nor do I finish my sentence out loud: *He used to like jelly beans.*

Instead, I change tracks:

I was raised to work hard and always do my best. At school, that meant being first in class. I also played the piano and danced ballet.

Back straight, shoulders back, ankles crossed. I pause to correct my posture on the gray suede couch.

My daughter takes ballet lessons,
she says.
She really likes them. Did you?
I loved them. I became a dancer.
A ballerina? How interesting.
Exhausting and demanding, actually. But it was what and who I wanted to be. I joined the corps de ballet when I was seventeen. . . .

I let the thought linger, midsentence, midair. I am disinclined to tell this stranger that I have not danced in years. I tell her instead about performances and plane rides to Toronto, Moscow, London, Vienna. Beirut, Geneva, Rome. Beijing, Istanbul, Santo Domingo, The Hague, San José, Tokyo. Catalonian beaches and Tuscan countrysides, the rickety old trams in Prague.

You have traveled a lot.
Yes.
So where is home?
Paris, always Paris.
Of course.

But you have been in the United States for . . .
Three years. Paris is still home.
I am perhaps a bit blunt.
I understand. What brought you here?
The man I married. Well, his work. Well, both.
And while he is at work, you dance here?
she asks. And the pretense is up.
Actually,
I work at a supermarket by our house,
just north of Furstenberg Street. I do not offer
more explanation. She, thankfully, does not ask.
You must miss it.
What, ballet or Paris? Both more than she can
imagine, but
I'd like to talk about something else now,
please.
Such as?
Anything.
Anorexia.
All right.
She moves on.
Let's start with your eating habits. Your file
says you are a vegetarian.
Vegan,
I rectify.
When did you make that transition?
I stopped eating meat at nineteen.
Why?
I am suddenly defensive:
Vegetarianism is not anorexia.

48

No it is not, you're right. I was just curious.
When did you become vegan?
When I came to America.
And why was that?
Because dairy tastes bad here.
Because dairy tastes different here.
What do you mean, bad?
I mean yogurt that contains fifteen ingredients,
thirteen of which I cannot pronounce,
I snap.
I also avoid processed foods, refined sugars,
high fructose corn syrup, and trans fats.
You don't find that extreme?
No. I find that healthy.

She makes no comment, but the irony of that
sentence is not lost on either of us.

I stare out the window for a while. She breaks
the silence first:

Was food an issue before you moved to the
States?
No.
Really?
Well . . .
What about your weight?
All dancers are careful not to gain too much
weight.
Were you?
Of course. The environment is very competitive.

Back straighter, ankles crossed the other
way.

She looks back at my chart:
But you were never overweight.
That is a relative term.
I mean to say your weight was average.
Silence.
Yes,
So was I.

12

She had opened the faucet so that the water would muffle any sound she made.

She was crying so hard she thought she would go blind, leaning into the bathroom wall. Her hands were pressed painfully against her face. She could not breathe or see, but she could not pull them away. She could not move. She could not stop shaking.

A sharp knock on the door.

She froze. She had thought no one had seen her leave the room.

Anna?

Not now, Philippe. She could not face him.

Un instant, Philippe.

She had not even told him about this evening; he had said he would be busy all week. He had said the black dress fit a bit too tight when she had tried it on for him. Now it did feel too tight and she felt fat and misshapen wearing it.

Anna!

Irritated rapping at the door. Hair, mascara back in place. Deep, concentrated breaths. She closed the faucet, pinched her cheeks so they were pink again. One last breath. She looked ahead, not seeing the creamy white marble, the fine gold frame around the mirror, the crystal chandelier above her head that matched those out in the hall.

She unlocked the door. He had not waited for her. Of course not. It would have appeared odd. She should not have come tonight. She would never have found out. She went back out into the crowded room.

Insipid, instrumental jazz was playing over the chatter. Waiters in bow ties were balancing trays of hors d'oeuvres and champagne. Ten minutes ago she had been part of this world of blinis and sparkling toasts. Then he had walked in, and not with her. The room had run out of air.

Now every blini in her stomach hurt. The acidity of the champagne. Her glass was where she had abandoned it in panic, on the window ledge by her purse. She looked straight at them, across the room. She needed her purse. And to leave.

She would say she was tired after the performance. She was.

Anna! You disappeared.

Their host, and Philippe. And the woman with whom he had walked in, her slender arm nestled in his.

Natasha, this is the girl I was telling you about. Anna, have you met Philippe's wife?

No she had not, but she had lost her voice,

52

*and her center of gravity. She stood, entranced
by Natasha, her black dress. It fit her perfectly.*

*Anna exchanged a kiss on each cheek with the
woman with long, sinewy legs. Her attention
was held by the smell of her perfume—orchids—
and Philippe's arm around her waist.*

Mademoiselle,

said the waiter,

blinis au caviar?

*But Anna's dress felt too tight. Anna's dress felt
too tight. His tray made her want to throw up.*

Non, merci.

And to Natasha, finally:

Enchantée.

Her fine chocolate hair, gold wedding band.

Excuse me, I was just leaving. I need to get
my purse.

And air.

13

Treatment Plan—May 23, 2016

Weight: 88 lbs.
BMI: 15.1

Diagnosis: Anorexia Nervosa. Restricting type.

Physiological Observations:
Malnutrition—severe. Potential for fluid and electrolyte imbalance. Hyponatremia. Amenorrhea. Osteopenia. Potential for cardiovascular instability. Bradycardia. Poor peripheral circulation—acrocyanosis. Abdominal bloating. Constipation.

Psychological/Psychiatric Observations:
Behavior consistent with manifestation of eating disorder. Symptoms of mild anxiety. Possible depression. Further assessment pending full examination by treatment team.

Summary:
Patient admitted to residential treatment on May 23, 2016. Team will work on improving

nutritional intake and nutritional variety, improving patient's body image and increasing her insight into the severity of her condition. Team will monitor for refeeding syndrome and work to achieve and maintain medical stability.

Given the severity of malnourishment and multiple medical concerns, residential treatment is indicated.

Treatment Objectives:
Resume normal nutrition, restore weight. Gradually increase caloric density and portion quantities.

Monitor vitals.
Monitor labs for refeeding syndrome and replenish electrolytes as indicated.
Prevent worsening of existing medical conditions.
Follow hormone levels.

Caloric Intake Target:
To be determined by nutritionist.

14

At 6:00 precisely, Direct Care knocks, signaling the end of the session. She escorts me from the therapist's office back to community space.

I observe her. She is by no standards thin. Her pants sit too snugly on her waist, a bit of skin protruding over the seams. Nothing too dramatic though, a normal woman's body. Just not one I would be caught dead in; the gap between standards and normalcy, and between this woman's body and the others in community space.

All the patients are there. There are seven of us, of whom five, including me, are anorexic. Not difficult to spot; they look pubescent and gaunt. Sunken eyes in sunken faces, scarecrow-thin arms and legs. Pale skin and hair, no lips. One is wearing a bright turquoise sweater. The color stands out.

Their ages are difficult to determine. As is mine, I suppose. They must be older than eighteen, at least; this is the women's center. But *women* rings false in my head. These patients are not women. They are missing breasts, curves, probably periods. Most are wearing children's clothes.

They look androgynous, their skin hanging in loose pockets around fragile frames. Not women; women have bodies, sex, lives, dinner, families. The patients in this room are girls with eyes that are too big.

I look at the other two girls, who seem less pale and emaciated than the rest. The skin around their mouths is dry and chapped, their knuckles are cracked and bruised. Bulimia, I guess. Less evident but just as lethal as anorexia. One of them is bobbing her head to music playing in her headphones.

They do not look like women either, though. I wonder why that is. Then I see the mismatch between their well-developed bodies and the adolescent anguish in their eyes.

Direct Care and the day team sign off; it is past 6:00 P.M. They take their purses, their silk scarves and car keys, and leave without saying goodbye. Those of us who remain do so in silence, with the night staff, trapped in this surreal, contrived environment and the diseases in our brains.

I had been warned that I would be overwhelmed by my first day in treatment; the information to be processed, the forms to be signed, the rules in the patient manual. Watching my tweezers, scissors, keys, and phone sealed away in storage bags. Being assigned a cubby, a bedroom, a seat at the table, a number.

But the warning had been inaccurate; the day

had unfolded smoothly. Until it ended and I sat down. Now for the first time today, I am still.

No one speaks to me, no one speaks. I realize that this is not a game. I am not going home tonight. I am having dinner, sleeping here.

Dusk and the panic settle and with those, my despair rises dangerously. I need to break the silence; I turn to the girl—one of the anorexics— next to me.

She is writing a letter on fine ivory paper. Left-handed, beautiful penmanship. I need her to be my friend.

Hello. My name is Anna.

She does not look up, but:

Valerie.

It helps. The heat in my chest begins to cool. Her name is Valerie.

I pause in that instant in which both our identities are still safely hazy. We do not have to be two girls with anorexia. We can just be Anna and Valerie. We can be two ladies chatting in a waiting room, any waiting room.

She continues writing. I watch her, discreetly. Her moving pen soothes me. She does not wear a wedding ring. A locket hangs around her neck. Her eyes are big and acorn brown. A nervous tick in the right one. We must be roughly the same age. She must have been beautiful, once.

I ransack my brain for a question, any question to move the conversation along. Most in

59

this setting seem inappropriate or irrelevant:

What brings you here? What do you do? How do you enjoy your free time?

Is there someone, something outside these walls waiting for you to come out?

I could, of course, fall back on logistics:

Is the staff agreeable?

Do you know if we are allowed to have coffee or chewing gum?

I could ask her for pointers or about pitfalls to avoid, but what I really want is reassurance.

Am I going to be okay?

But she seems engrossed in her writing and my courage is faltering.

I fall back into the seat and the silence. She signs her letter and folds it. Then, the receiver's name:

To Anna.

She hands it to me. I am stunned.

Inside:

I'm so glad you are here. You seem nice. I hope we become good friends. You'll soon see I'm nuttier than squirrel poop, but don't let me scare you away.

Don't let any of us, or this place. It's not as impossible as it seems. It will be all right, don't worry. We will all help.

Valerie

She does not look nuttier than squirrel poop. She just looks very sad. And like most anorexics she looks like she is trying to starve the feeling out. Odd that she would mention a squirrel; she reminds me of one. Petite and fragile, her soft light brown hair in a bun, the way I put up mine.

P.S. Here are a few of the house rules.

My brain springs to attention. This set of rules is different from the one I received at orientation.

Emm will surely go over them with you. She is the leader of our group.

I do not know who Emm is, yet, but I assume I will soon.

I read on, curious. The manifesto begins with:

All girls are to be patient with one another.
No girl left at the table alone,
because we are all in this together.

Composure is to be maintained in front of any guests to the house.

Horoscopes are to be read and taken seriously every morning over breakfast.

Copies of the daily word jumbles are to be distributed at that time. The group has all day to solve them. Answers disclosed at evening snack.

Note writing and passing is encouraged. No note must fall into Direct Care's hands.

Books, music, letter paper, postage stamps, and flowers received are to be shared.

An odd rule follows:

The availability of cottage cheese is to be celebrated every Tuesday, because, I suppose, in a place like this, all occasions to celebrate must be seized.

as are animal crackers, the morning walks, and any excursions on Saturday.

She ends on a more serious tone:

No one will ever judge, tell on, or cause any suffering to the rest.

And I hope you don't mind, this last one is personal: I like the corner spot on the couch.

I smile. *All right, Valerie. The corner spot is yours.*

There are more rules but I forgot them. For more information, ask Emm.

The panic has subsided, for now. I want to thank Valerie but one glance her way reveals it is not a good time; her eye is twitching, her hands are clenched. A few minutes later, I understand why. Direct Care walks in and announces:

Almost six thirty, ladies. Everybody stand up.

It is dinnertime.

15

Matthias and Anna were the only adults in the queue whose presence was not legitimized by children. They did not mind. They giggled, like children. How else was one to spend such a gorgeous Sunday in April?

This had been one of their first dates: a theme park. Merry-go-round, ice cream of course, and roller-coaster rides. Also a valuable lesson they had learned: never to be done in that order.

They were older and wiser this time, and married for a full year too. Tickets scanned, admission was granted into the magical kingdom. They took one cheeky look at one another and ran toward their first ride. A fork in the yellow brick road: Batman or Superman first?

Obviously, Batman.

It was a little chilly, but Anna had brought Matthias's sweatshirt with her just in case. She slipped it on gratefully as they waited for their turn to ride.

Anna, you can't possibly be cold.

Matthias was sweating profusely. Everyone around them was too.

Well, she was, not cold necessarily, just

uncomfortable with the light breeze. Even the temperature of Matthias's cool hand had made her pull away. The sweatshirt helped, and she did not care what the people around them thought anyway.

The queue edged forward.

Batman, baby!

Batman, baby,

she echoed.

Except there was a knot in her stomach, and there were palpitations in her chest. Anna was not afraid of roller coasters. Anna was not afraid of anything. Anna was the girl who went on all the rides and tried every new thing at least once. She had been skydiving, caving, mountain climbing, cliff hanging, and snow-boarding with Matthias. Anna was the girl who went snowboarding with her husband, she reminded herself again. Still, the knot in her stomach. And it was their turn to ride. Too late.

It started wrong. The jolt forward made her neck snap, then her head slam back into the seat. It bobbed and banged against everything uncontrollably like the loose head of a Chinese fortune cat.

The train stopped at the top for a split-second release before dipping at vertiginous speed. Matthias screamed and Anna screamed. It was not the same scream. Her organs had been left *behind, at the top, her vertebrae were being knocked around. At a sharp angle, her hip hit the seat on the right. And the wind, that horrible wind . . .*

Anna! Hands in the air, I dare you!

But Anna was otherwise occupied; if she let go her arms would be yanked out of their sockets, no match for the ride's speed.

Screeching halt. Thank God. She could barely get out of her seat. She looked around; everyone around her was laughing, applauding. Matthias was hopping with excitement. He took her by the arm and pulled her along as he skipped like a child. It hurt.

Shall we go again? Shall we go on the Superman? That was incredible! Let's . . . Anna, is everything okay?

No, everything hurt. Everything made her dizzy. Everything was hard and cold. That ride had been pure torture. How on earth had she once liked roller coasters?

Everything is fine!

Even she knew that sounded fake.

I am just a little nauseated from the ride.

And probably, from having been fasting since last night. She had had to, preemptively, knowing that Matthias would want to have ice cream today. And fries. Matthias and Anna went on roller-coaster rides together and shared ice cream and fries.

Go on the next one without me. I just need to rest a little.

What? Of course not! I'll wait. We can sit here till you feel a little better, then go on the next ride together.

Matthias—

No way. Not without you. Don't worry, we have plenty of time. Believe me, by the time the park closes we will have gone on each ride twice!

To nausea was added panic: how would she survive the day? It was only noon and the park closed at nine, and the next ride, she was sure, would break her ribs.

Matthias and Anna loved roller coasters.

I love roller coasters, she reminded herself. To Matthias, she said,

All right, Superman. I am ready! Let's ride.

No one else seemed distraught in the queue on that sunny Sunday. Anna plastered on her biggest smile, and when their train arrived, pulled the metal guard as far down on her chest as it would go.

I love roller coasters. I love roller coasters.

Jerk. Propulsion. Dive, turn, loop, bang, bang.

I love roller coasters.

A sharp pain in her pelvis. She was crying.

Make it stop!

Matthias went on the rest of the rides alone, and they did not have ice cream that day. Anna blamed it on the nausea. Matthias said nothing. They went home.

The next morning there were big black and blue bruises on her thighs, arms, and behind. Matthias said nothing then either, except that he was late for work.

Matthias and Anna used to love roller coasters, but after that April Sunday, Anna announced that theme parks had become a little too crowded for her taste. The music was too loud. The roller coasters redundant. Even good ice cream was hard to find. Matthias could have said something then, but he did not. What difference would it have made?

They had both become too comfortably settled in the magical kingdom of make-believe. She made believe that she was happy and all was fine and he made believe it was true. It was less painful than confrontation. Confrontation just led to fights.

And so she ate nothing and they both ate lies through three years of marriage, for peace, at the occasional cost of no more roller coasters, no more sharing ice cream and French fries.

16

We stand in line, two by two, for the brief walk to the adjacent house. There dinner will be served, my first meal here. My feet do not want to move. I glance at the rest of the girls; most of them do not seem to be faring much better. We must look comical; seven grown women like schoolgirls in two straight lines, waiting to be taken to dinner. No, we look sad; seven grown women in two straight lines, waiting to be taken to dinner.

I fold and hold on to Valerie's note. The girls ahead of me begin to walk. No turning back now. I am scared but do not even know what to expect.

We cross the lawn from 17 Swann Street to the yellow house next door. The girl in the turquoise sweatshirt is in front. I conclude she must be Emm.

She leads us into the dining room. My eyes and trust settle on her. She seems oddly calm for an anorexic at dinner. Her turquoise soothes me.

I focus on her hair: spectacular, cascading. An anorexic abnormality. Enormous eyes, fierce beauty. An athlete's posture, if not build. She must have been a swimmer or a gymnast, I guess. Not anymore, though; two matchsticks for legs.

She walks up to me and speaks. Introductions:

Hello, my name is Emily. Everybody here calls me Emm.

Her warmth is professional and precisely titrated, like that of a customer-service agent.

I'm so glad you are here. Please feel free to reach out if I can do anything to help.

Were she not so painfully thin underneath that giant sweatshirt, I would have mistaken her for staff. Were her face not so painfully devoid of emotion, I would have mistaken her for genuine. *I'm so glad you are here.* She seems indifferent at best. Tired too, like Valerie. Late twenties, I guess. Again the dissonance: old woman's face, child's body.

The clock on the wall announces: six thirty. Direct Care announces:

Let's eat!

The anticipation that had been gnawing at my stomach has developed into pain. The acrid fear now grates throughout my insides; the result is corrosive and hot.

There are two round tables in the room; our names are on one or the other. Every girl locates hers and takes a seat.

Our plates are already set in front of us, wrapped in plastic and ominous. I am not ready; I know that if I look at mine I will panic. My stomachache has, I think, developed into a proper ulcer. Distraction, I need a distraction. I look around at the other girls.

Valerie first, but she is in no state to offer me reassurance; the cook hands her what looks like a frozen orange. Wordlessly, roughly, she grabs it. She digs her nails deep into the flesh; my first exposure to a grounding technique. She will clutch the orange for the rest of the meal and eat with her other hand.

Within minutes, other odd behaviors emerge. One girl taps her foot anxiously. It makes the unsteady table shake and the rest of us even more jittery. Another girl proceeds to cut a piece of potato into paper-thin slivers. I squirm; the gesture is too familiar for comfort. I do that with my food too.

Too small, Katerina. You know that,
says Direct Care, watching over us like a warden.

Emm has not started. She is still examining every piece of her silverware, wiping it methodically with a paper napkin and placing it neatly on the table.

Do what you like, Emm, but remember: this is the only napkin you'll get.
Nonplussed, she carefully peels the plastic wrap covering her first course, folds it carefully, places it to her right. Calm? Or obsessive-compulsive? Or just delaying having to eat?

71

Forty-five minutes and not one more, ladies.
Silent tension answers Direct Care.
Julia, you can't possibly be done already!
Julia objects:
Hey! I was hungry!
I stare at the girl and her empty plate, dumb-struck. Mine is still untouched in front of me.

She turns toward the kitchen and calls to the cook:

Great job, Rita! Man, I was starved! I'd have seconds if I could,
pointed glare at Direct Care,
but I'm not allowed.
After a period of acclimation to this odd little dinner affair, conversation slowly, painfully picks up. To my surprise, it gains momentum. It flows almost normally from the weather to current, random events, a brief exchange of backgrounds, interests, a few photographs of children and pets. Stories of jobs and trips and a life prior to here are shared. I begin to loosen up. But every few minutes Direct Care interrupts the pretense:

Stop spreading that sauce around your plate, Chloe. You'll have to scoop it up at the end. No, Julia, you cannot help her finish her rice. And no! You cannot taste!
Once, twice,
All the cheese and salad dressing, ladies. Come on, you all know the rules.

Conversation becomes difficult to rekindle. The group lapses into sad silence.

Dessert will bring down even more walls, I am sure, but dessert has not been served yet.

Thirty minutes, Anna,

Direct Care reminds me. I have not even begun!

I cannot afford any more delays. I look down at my plate; the plastic wrap covers half a bagel and some hummus, with carrots, yogurt, and fruit. Some of these foods I have not eaten in years. *I cannot eat all of this!* I cannot eat any of this. Protest? Refuse? Make a scene? Leave the room? Where would I go?

Direct Care is looking at me. I have no choice. Eyes on my plate, brain far away. I reach for a carrot but panic and bile rise in spite of me up to my throat.

This is it: *You will eat whatever is put on your plate,* I was told. But I cannot. I am not a quitter, but I cannot do this. I cannot breathe. I cannot breathe.

Anna, do you watch TV shows?

The voice belongs to Emm, sitting across from me, her back to the dining room wall, cutting her food, one bite at a time, chewing pensively, thoroughly. Her question is so outrageously mundane it dissipates the noise in my head. I cannot eat this meal but I can answer that question.

Very few, in fact, but I grew up in the nineties; I am a devoted fan of Friends.

That's my favorite show of all time! My other passion is the Olympics.

I understand what she is doing for me, her cruise-director smile on. This girl is not the kind to unfold a personal life at the table. She does not mention a dog, career, family, but she does talk, at length, about *Friends*. As she does I mirror her picking up a baby carrot and dipping it into the hummus.

Dinner progresses. *Just focus on Emm.* Bite, chew, swallow. Emm. She chatters on and I wonder how she manages to eat at the same time. I make it through the carrots and hummus, and even, with a lot of water, the bagel. I am not thinking, just chewing and picturing episode after episode of *Friends*.

The fruit is fine, but I hit a wall at the yogurt. I do not eat dairy. *Please, Direct Care.* I turn to her, ready to beg, but before I can Emm interjects:

Do you like word games?

I suppose I do.

We have word jumbles every day at breakfast.

But as it is dinner, she has charades on hand.

Let's see what you've got, Anna. Consider this your rite of passage. Prepare to be hazed.

Julia chortles, but Emm, with utmost serious-nous quizzes me. My mind still on the yogurt, I fail miserably at the first two charades.

Come on, Anna! Concentrate,

Emm chides, as she scoops up a spoonful of her own yogurt. *Come on, Anna.* I imitate her gesture and focus my thoughts on her clues.

I solve the third charade. Applause around the table. And in my head. I take a few more bites. Emm appears not to notice and quizzes me through the rest.

Her own assigned meal is huge and I worry she will not be able to finish it. But if she is distraught, she does not show it, just checks the clock from time to time. By the end of the forty-five minutes, my meal is eaten. Hers is too. We put our spoons down. Dinner is over. Emm, like a switch, turns quiet.

She almost looks calm. I almost believe it. Direct Care says,

Ladies! Two lines.

17

The girls disperse when we reach the house. The atmosphere is one of quiet mourning. Except for Julia who, bulimia and headphones blaring, informs us that she is still hungry.

Valerie is in her spot on the couch, crying softly. No one disturbs her. Every girl for herself now, fighting her own demons, waiting for the guilt to dissipate.

Emm takes a book and sits on the stairs, away from the rest of the group. She clearly wants to be left alone, but I approach her nonetheless.

Thank you,

I say, standing there awkwardly, wishing I had come better prepared.

You did fine back there. You'll be fine,

she says.

Her voice businesslike and detached.

The course of treatment for anorexia is painful but not impossible. If you really want to recover, you will.

At this very instant I really want to take my anorexia and run away. But I do not tell her that, or anything, still unable to say something smart.

She speaks again instead:

Again, if you have any questions at all, do not hesitate to ask.

Clearly an effort to end this conversation and return to her reading. Except I do, finally, have a question:

How do you know I will be fine?

She looks up from her book, no longer emotionless. The saddest smile and answer follow:

Because I've seen girls like you get better. I've been here for four years.

18

I am back in community space and my stomach hurts.

Once upon a time I used to eat. I even used to like to eat. I used to bake the best *tarte aux pêches* and dunk crackers in my cocoa or tea, and flip heavenly, airy crêpes with my eyes closed. I had a secret recipe for *Sacher torte*. I used to savor fresh, hot croissants on Sunday mornings with Matthias.

I used to eat. I used to like to eat, then I grew scared to eat, ceased to eat. Now my stomach hurts; I have been anorexic so long that I have forgotten how to eat.

Dinner is over, my first real meal in years. But the anxiety has just begun. It is 7:28. The day is settling down but my feet, heart, and mind are racing.

Direct Care says:

Anna, sit down please. Stop pacing like that. You're making everybody uncomfortable.

But I cannot. I am going to be sick.

I need to step outside.

You cannot.

79

No, I cannot breathe. I cannot stay indoors, sit down, or stop pacing. Or do this. I want my anorexia back! I want to leave!

The clock hits 7:30. The doorbell rings.

19

Matthias is standing at the door, clean shaven, hair handsomely combed, holding a red rose and looking extremely ill at ease. He is wearing a crisp blue shirt that I like, one I had ironed last week. Last week. Another world and time away, neither of which seems real.

For an instant I stand, stunned, expecting him to disappear when I blink. He does not. I blink again, just in case. Then I fly into his arms.

I am touching Matthias. Hugging Matthias as though I have not seen him in forever. It has been forever since he dropped me off here only a few hours ago. The heat from his chest. I had forgotten the rhythm of his heart on my ear. My husband holds me stiffly, unpleasantly aware that we are being watched.

A curious crew of six pale girls and Direct Care stand behind me. I do not notice them, too busy showering him with kisses and questions:

What are you doing here? I cannot believe this! Are you allowed to be here?

When I finally let him he hands me the rose that is now less crimson than his face, and says in a flushed voice:

They told me visiting hours were at seven thirty.

Visiting hours. Visiting hours! How had I not registered that? I must have misplaced that piece of information in the pile I was given at orientation. I ask Direct Care:

How much time do I have?

Ninety minutes,

she says,

till I call you for the evening snack. You may not go outside unsupervised yet, but you may go to your room.

I am so happy I do not even revolt against the house rules; that I am twenty-six and have just been told that I "may" take my husband to my room. The rules of the real world do not apply here, in the house at 17 Swann Street. I accept that, for now; I only have eighty-nine minutes with Matthias left.

Then a sobering realization: it is past seven thirty. I look at the front door and back at the other girls. No other visitor is here. Suddenly I feel inconsiderate for having kissed Matthias in public. I push him back gently, and with an effort at *retenue*, take him upstairs to my room.

Our restraint lasts until he closes the door of the Van Gogh room . . . then we kick our shoes off and race toward the bed. We kiss till we are both out of breath.

You bought me a rose,

I finally say.

I missed you,
he replies.
I missed you,
I say and realize that I no longer have a stomachache.

He touches my fingers. They are cold. He rubs them, my hands, my feet. I massage his shoulders and neck, pressing at the points I know are always tense. Both acts feel delicately, painfully familiar. We used to do this all the time; spend hours kissing, touching one another, tracing maps on each other's skin.

I am not sure exactly when we stopped. Perhaps before Christmas last year. It had come gradually. Less, then less time spent kissing, touching. Matthias had blamed his exhaustion after work, the weather, perhaps a flu. I had believed him because it had suited me. I had no interest in, energy for sex.

How did your first day go?
he asks.
Tell me everything.
I scrunch my nose. I say,
You go first.
He counters,
We'll take turns. You start.
So I do, with dinner, the only concrete achievement to report. I tell him I ate hummus, a bagel, some carrots, and yogurt. He stares at me in disbelief:

You ate all of that, Anna?

He kisses me and I decide, perhaps prematurely, that eating dinner was worth it.

Now your turn.

He tells me he searched everywhere for the coffee this afternoon. To which I reply:

Left cupboard. Second shelf. The tin with a red lid.

I tell him about orientation, the other girls, my first meeting with the therapist. He tells me about the drive to work after leaving me here. The hollow apartment at six in the evening made worse by the missing coffee. Television and cereal for dinner, from the box. I ask him what he watched. He cannot remember. It does not matter. Then we just hold hands.

He breaks the silence first:

How do I determine where my side of the bed ends and yours begins?

I hear the question he is not asking. The answer is: *I do not know.* I do not know if we will be okay. I want to tell him we will. I want to reassure and comfort this man, this boy sitting on my bed. I answer in the same code:

I left you a container of spaghetti with mushrooms in the fridge.

The trouble with visiting hours, the trouble with happiness, is that time ticks and both end. Our treacherous ninety minutes fly over us as we just sit on the bed. A glance at his watch and Matthias begins lacing up his first shoe. He pauses to look at me:

This reminds me of when we first started dating.

I remember us then. The little cupboard room we lived in, the student stipend we lived on. The novelty of his smell. The first time he put his arm on my chest and fell asleep; the reassuring weight of him.

He turns to his second shoe and I to the photograph of that first morning on the whiteboard.

You look like you did in that photograph. Do you remember that morning?

He looks at it and me and us and neither of us says, out loud, that life has changed, we have both changed since that photograph.

He is brave and quiet and I know that he is returning to an empty home. To whatever cereal is still in the box and a container of spaghetti. Because of me, tonight, for the first time in years, we will both go to bed alone.

I stop his shoelace tying and kiss him on the lips, nose, cheeks, collarbones, eyelids and lashes, chest. I kiss him enough to last him, I hope, until visiting hours tomorrow.

For a second, we are not in Bedroom 5 of the house at 17 Swann Street. For a second we are in that photograph. Then Matthias pulls away and we are back.

Date tomorrow night?

I will be here.
And the night after that, and after that?
I will still be here.
Matthias leaves at 9:00 P.M.

I had been instructed during orientation not to open my bedroom window. *Flight and suicide prevention,* Direct Care had explained. Well, I am not going anywhere, not if Matthias is coming tomorrow. I open the window rebelliously and watch our blue car drive away.

I think of Matthias in our studio apartment, on pause in our bed and our life. I think of Van Gogh in my Van Gogh room. Open windows at the Saint-Paul asylum. Starry, starry nights and flower shops. Then Direct Care comes by:

Time for the evening snack. The other girls have started. And close that window, Anna.

20

You can always tell when Matthias and Anna are nearby.

General chuckle.

Ah bon?

Oui, just listen closely and follow the little kissing sounds.

Anna turned tomato red, but both she and Matthias laughed. They had to admit Frédéric had a point. They were always making kissing sounds.

Are we one of those couples?

she asked.

We are,

Matthias replied solemnly.

Anna, we are one of those annoying couples that make everyone around them cringe.

They were Matthias and Anna, Anna and Matthias, who were so often busy kissing that they forgot their keys at home and their bags at the supermarket. They consistently missed their stop while riding the Métro and elicited disapproving clicks from proper old ladies on the sidewalk.

Their friends found it amusing, fortunately.

They were having apéritifs, warming up for one last party before Matthias left tomorrow for "l'Amérique!"

You never kiss me like he kisses her,

Marianne pouted to Frédéric, to which he immediately responded with a loud caricatured smack on the lips. She pushed him back, scowling; it did not count. But Frédéric, ever good-humored, said,

Chérie, no one kisses like that forever. They are still newlyweds. You and I have been together for ten years! Wait and see, the honeymoon will end. They will grow up and out of all that kissing.

And to Matthias and Anna:

You should learn from Marianne and me. We do not kiss anymore. We fight! It keeps things interesting, as you can see. You should try it.

The group laughed. Frédéric poured himself some more wine. He then slid by Marianne on the couch and tried to cajole her into forgiveness. It took a second glass, and some deeper, longer kissing, but he eventually won.

Matthias filled his own glass again and touched it lightly against Anna's. Then his lips touched hers. They both tasted of alcohol and its sweet woody texture.

I don't think I will grow out of kissing you.

I do not think I will either.

Let's not become like Frédéric and Marianne.

No. Let's go home and make love.

Matthias looked at Anna, surprised. She was not normally the brazen one. She misread his expression and, flustered, recovered:

I mean . . . we do not have to—

He laughed.

No we don't. We want to. I want to. I don't know why we are still here. Get your coat.

They lingered for a few minutes, all they could manage, then slipped out as more wine was being poured. They would not be missed.

And if we are,

Matthias said,

Frédéric will just joke about it next time.

21

At 8:00 A.M. sharp, we take our seats in the breakfast area downstairs. A long wooden table, my first breakfast, my second day here. I have been up since 5:00 A.M.

Trying to keep calm, I pray for coffee. There is coffee. I can do this. Too soon; I see breakfast, half a bagel and cream cheese, wrapped in plastic, land in front of me.

This has to be someone's idea of a joke. I see no humor in it. I had not wanted to be difficult last night, when yogurt had been served at dinner, but my file clearly states that I am a vegan. Something must be said.

There must be a mistake. I do not eat dairy,
I inform Direct Care as politely as I can. Perhaps I naively expect a waiter to swoop into the room, apologize elegantly for the misunderstanding, and remove my plate.

Valerie puts her spoon down and her hand on the edge of the table.

You will eat whatever the nutritionist has set,
Direct Care replies. Period.

Tuesday's breakfast is a bagel and cream cheese. No exceptions to the menu.

She turns her attention to the other girls. My name stares at my horrified face, printed neatly in thick black felt right on the plastic wrap. There is no mistake, and this is not a joke. No one is laughing, least of all me.

Quite the opposite. I am angry now. I had tried to cooperate. I had eaten dinner last night like all the other girls and had not caused a scene. I had played along with my treatment team's game, but they had taken it too far. I push the plate away with as much cold disdain as I can muster.

No cream cheese and bagel for me, thank you. I would like a word with the manager.

I would like a word with the nutritionist please. Direct Care looks unfazed.

Now, you will complete or refuse your breakfast. As for speaking with the nutritionist, you may do that on the day and time at which your session with her has been assigned.

Officially, I am outraged. Secretly, terrified. My façade remains cool, I hope, but beneath it disaster bubbles dangerously. I try to remain calm, but I have crossed the twenty-four-hour good-behavior threshold. I can feel everyone around the table tensing but do not care at this point.

I would like to speak to the nutritionist now. Keep calm. Inhale. Exhale.

Are you refusing to complete your breakfast?

Yes, that is exactly what I am doing. I am an adult. Here by choice. Free to leave as I please. To prove it, I stand up as calmly as my shaking knees will allow and walk away from the table.

Much happens simultaneously.

Julia tries to steal a few sweeteners from the table. She is apprehended by the nurse. All the girls jump, one of them spills her coffee. Quiet Valerie bursts into sobs.

And I, the reason behind all this chaos, do not make it very far. In fact, not even out of the breakfast area before Direct Care grabs me by the arm. I contemplate further escalation of the conflict. She appears to do the same. She makes the decision for us both after a few seconds of tug-of-war:

You have two refusals left, after which you'll get a feeding tube. If you want to see the nutritionist, return to your seat and I'll see if she's in her office.

The thought of the yellow feeding tube running through my nostrils and down my throat, pumping dense and beige liquid food into my stomach, chills me in place. Not the feeding tube. *Please,* not the feeding tube. I have seen those in hospitals before, yellow lines that get taped to the cheek and go straight into the patient's stomach. I fight the image in my head and a powerful gagging reflex.

Yes, please do,

I say calmly, lowering my telltale trembling chin.

I am escorted back to my seat, where I have full view of the damage I have caused. I disrupted breakfast, got Julia in trouble, and at the very least made everyone uncomfortable. Valerie is given her frozen orange to clutch. Only Emm is still reading the word jumbles.

I feel horrible. I want to apologize to the girls, but I have done enough for one breakfast. 8:30 A.M. comes and goes. The plates are cleared. The girls stand up and leave the room.

I and my untouched half bagel and cream cheese are instructed to remain. An apprehensive, waiting-room sort of dread. Direct Care informs me she spoke to my nutritionist. She will see me at 9:00 A.M.

At nine I am led to her office and told to wait on the couch. This one is plush and red. Too comfortable. I do not relax.

The portly lady who enters the room next I dislike instantly. Too much makeup, jewelry, perfume. Too much skin. Every bit of her is too much.

She goes straight to the point:

I'm Allison, your nutritionist. What did you want to see me about?

She has not even bothered to smile. We are not going to get along.

So this disagreeable lady and her pout were

94

responsible for my meals so far. Her job is to make me gain weight. Well, our goals are already opposed. I assess this Allison who in the future will dictate every calorie pumped into my stomach. I try not to look terrified.

Keep it polite, elegant, professional, I tell myself in my head.

I would like to discuss the menu with you, please. I cannot eat the food you are serving me.

She finally smiles, just not a smile that bodes very well for me. My stomach is churning, but I try to hold my ground.

I am vegan; I do not eat cream cheese. Nor do I think a bagel is a nutritious breakfast choice. I am open to eating muesli as a healthier breakfast alternative, if you would like to discuss that. Fruits are fine, and as for lunch—

Let me interrupt you right there,

she says. My bravado dissipates.

I'm not interested in your views on nutrition. I went to college for those. I'm here to make you gain weight, and fast. You will eat what you're served.

I stare at her in disbelief. No one has ever addressed me like that. But I do not have time to react because she carries on:

You will follow a weight-gain meal plan. The goal is two to four pounds a week. Your portions and caloric intake will be increased gradually.

You will meet with me on a biweekly basis so I can determine those, and in between you will be closely monitored for symptoms of refeeding syndrome.

Refeeding syndrome. Potentially fatal shifts in fluids and electrolyte levels, like sudden drops of phosphate in the blood, when a malnourished patient is refed. Starving bodies that have starved for too long can quite literally be shocked by food. Muscle weakness, coma, possibly death.

She knows she now has my attention.

The nutritionist continues:

You will be given the chance to choose all your meals once a week. We usually offer our patients two options, but since you're vegetarian—

Vegan,

I try again.

We do not accommodate vegans. Now, as I was saying . . . Since you're vegetarian, you will only have one nonmeat option to choose from.

What if I do not like that nonmeat option?

Then you will have a substitute meal like the one you had for dinner yesterday.

What if I do not like the substitute?

I am irritating her, but this is too horrifyingly important for me to let up. She sighs and closes her eyes, and when she opens them again, speaks in a sickly sweet voice I immediately recognize as dangerous:

You don't know what you like or don't like, not that it matters at this point.

I beg her pardon?

That smile again. In the same sickly voice, but with an eyebrow lifted, she asks:

How do you take your coffee?

Black. No sugar.

How do you take your tea?

Hot. Green or ginger.

Sugar?

Of course not.

How do you take your eggs?

I do not like eggs.

How do you butter your toast?

I do not butter my toast.

I do not eat butter or toast. No fats or simple carbohydrates.

Milk or dark chocolate?

Neither, thank you.

What do you like to eat?

What do you eat? would have been a simpler question to answer. I eat fruits, apples mostly. Sometimes with a squeeze of lemon. When I want something salty I eat lettuce or cabbage. For a treat: microwave popcorn.

What do you like to eat?

I have not answered her. Apples and popcorn, I suppose. Once upon a time my answer to that question would have been very different. Once upon a time I also would have told her that I ate my eggs scrambled, chocolate dark, toast warm and just barely crisp and golden. No butter but sprinkled with salt.

But now I do not like to eat anything. I eat out of necessity, to silence my hunger and function a while longer.

Apples and popcorn
do the trick. I do not need or want anything else, her horrible bagels and cream cheese.

I would like to order off the menu please. Something healthy and natural, something like—
Popcorn?
she interrupts. Her patience and even her fake, thread-thin smile have run out.

You would need to eat thirty-five bags a day, or forty-six point sixty-six medium apples to meet your caloric needs.

She has succeeded, again, in shocking me into silence. I do not understand what she means. Rather, I do not want to understand what she means by "caloric needs."

Let me explain the refeeding process to you, who seem to know so much about nutrition:

A normal body, at rest, needs a thousand calories to survive. Just the basics: heartbeat, breath, blood flow, body temperature.

I already wince at a thousand.

A normal woman of your height and age needs a thousand to fifteen hundred more to carry out the basic active functions of her day: like getting out of bed, going to work. Driving her car, talking on the phone, picking up groceries, walking the dog, hanging her coat up, even watching TV . . . but you need even more than that.

More? *More?* Than *two thousand calories?* More than *two thousand five hundred?*

Because you've been starving and overexercising, you've been feeding on your own organs. You have no fat reserves, no period, no calcium in your bones. No estradiol in your bloodstream. In fact, you are less woman now than a two-year-old girl.

She is treating me like that two-year-old girl, the recurring theme of this place. But I have no time to be angry; the nutritionist drops her next bomb:

In order to repair the damage you've done, your body needs more energy. More energy means more calories: five hundred more, at least.

I do the math, poorly, in my head. I feel a panic attack coming on.

Two thousand five hundred calories?

I shriek.

At least. Probably more. I have had patients consume up to three thousand five hundred for results.

Three thousand five hundred calories! A day! More food than I consume in four! She is mad, utterly mad.

You need low-volume, high-fat, calorie-dense foods. Believe me, thirty-five bags of popcorn will not fit in that stomach of yours.

I do not even bother to hold back the tears. The time is past for pretense at poise. I cry like that two-year-old girl, terrified and trapped in a body I have no use for.

I do not scream. I hiccup and sob. I tell her to go to hell and that I am done. I am taking my anorexia with me and we are both going home.

If you leave you will die,

she says, indifferent, bringing this conversation to an end. She walks past the plush red chair and opens the door. Our first session is over.

And keep in mind that you have two refusals left before you get the tube.

22

Meal Plan—May 24, 2016

Patient Body Mass Index: 15.1
Normal BMI range: 18.5–24.9

Other symptoms:
Bradycardia, arrhythmias, osteopenia, unstable vital signs.

Treatment Objective:
Weight gain and restoration of patient BMI to within normal range.

Meal Plan:
Patient will consume three meals and three snacks at two-to-three-hour intervals daily.

Initial caloric value set at 2,100 calories per day, to be increased by 250–300 calories every forty-eight hours to seventy-two hours.

Patient will be monitored for symptoms of refeeding syndrome and other medical complications, including but not limited to: heart failure, arrhythmias, respiratory failure, muscle breakdown, sudden death.

Calorie Guidelines (to be revised as needed)

Breakfast: 400 calories (to be increased to 800 calories)

Lunch: 550 calories (to be increased to 800–1,000 calories)

Dinner: 550 calories (to be increased to 800–1,000 calories)

Midmorning snack: 200 calories (to be increased to 400 calories)

Afternoon snack: 200 calories (to be increased to 400 calories)

Evening snack: 200 calories (to be increased to 400 calories)

Meal Plan may be complemented by a liquid nutritional supplement to increase calorie density. Value: 350 calories per 8 fl. oz. Liquid supplement must be administered immediately if meals are skipped, refused, or unfinished.

23

I am back in community space before 10:00 A.M. I try to breathe down the storm in my chest; I have cried enough for today, for the week, and it is only Tuesday.

Only two days, and I am already suffocating in this place, from being told when and what to eat, when to use the bathroom and when to go to sleep. Two days ago I was a grown woman. Now I have two refusals left. I must have signed my independence off on one of those admission forms.

All the women who come here do, with the keys, phones, and tweezers they hand in. They also sign off their lives, careers, families, closets of dresses and high heels. Stripped of the energy to process anything beyond heartbeat, breathing, some body heat, they then devolve into little girls throwing tantrums at breakfast tables.

What a mess and first impression I made this morning in front of the other girls. Most do not even know my name yet. They are now out on their morning walk.

I must apologize as soon as they return. The front door opens and they enter.

Emm comes straight to me and in her professional voice, asks if she can have a word.

I follow her to the alcove underneath the stairs. She climbs into it and sits on the floor, motioning me to join. Her manner is so natural I know she has had meetings like this here before.

I understand how difficult this morning was for you,

she begins before I can,

but you disrupted breakfast. Everyone in here is suffering, and everyone is suffering enough.

She speaks quietly and kindly. It strikes deeper than if she had been upset. The frozen orange, the sweetener, the silence at the table. One of the rules of the house: *to be kind.*

I open my mouth to apologize but she cuts me off before I can:

It's okay, and so are the others. We don't hold grudges here. We each lived our own first forty-eight hours in this house. Just focus on surviving yours.

She pauses.

It will get easier after that. At least then you get the morning walk.

Yes, I remember Direct Care saying that. Forty-eight hours in and pending good behavior. Only twenty-four more to go.

I am sorry,

I say lamely anyway as she climbs out of the alcove.

No need,
she calls over her shoulder.

Twenty-four hours left. I can focus on surviving this place till then.

Then I notice Direct Care setting the table: midmorning snack, already.

I am not ready yet. I have no choice. We all flock toward the breakfast table. I keep my eyes down, still embarrassed by my earlier behavior. Two bowls and a plate are placed in front of me. All three wrapped in plastic and labeled.

The first contains yogurt. Vanilla. The second has animal crackers.

In spite of me, of the horror of the situation, I suddenly want to chuckle. In my head, I hear the first lines of a poem I used to know and love:

Animal crackers and cocoa to drink,
That is one of the finest of suppers I think.

My mother's voice is reciting the words. I am five and in the kitchen with her. The cocoa is steaming in its wide white bowl, warming me on a rainy school night. My animal crackers are waiting patiently for their turn to be dipped until just soft. They did not scare me then. That memory is a happy one.

I then turn to the plate, confused. I do not understand, till I do: my uneaten half bagel and cream cheese, this morning's breakfast I had refused.

I choke; I am expected to eat it now, and my

midmorning snack too. The girls around me, even Direct Care, are quiet, waiting for me to react.

Yogurt, and crackers, and the bagel and cream cheese. I try to rein in my breaths. . . .

And hyperventilate.

My body is screaming: *Not all at once! Please!* The nutritionist's voice responds: *You have two refusals left.* And Emm's, who is sitting across from me: *Everyone is suffering enough.*

Every girl is to be kind. I cannot make a scene. But I cannot do this! *Please . . .*

The animal crackers in the bowl. I hear the poem again. Somehow, my mother's quiet voice drowns out all the others in my head. It trails along rhythmically, soothingly slowing the pace of my inhales and exhales:

Animal crackers and cocoa to drink,
That is one of the finest of suppers I think.

This is ridiculous. I am twenty-six years old and reciting a children's poem. But it helps, if only with the breathing. I continue, in my head:

When I'm grown up and can have what I please
I think I shall always insist upon these.

I cannot refuse this meal. I wish Maman were here. I wish I were anywhere, anywhere but here. How did the poem go?

Focus on the next line. And on unwrapping the bagel. Now the cream cheese. Spread. Take a bite. And another bite. Chew. *Do not think, keep your brain on the poem.*

What do you choose when you're offered a treat?

When Mother says, "What would you like best to eat?"

Swallow. Drink water. Start again. One more bite. And another, and another after that.

Is it waffles and syrup, or cinnamon toast?

Keep chewing to the end of the stanza. I swallow the last bite of bagel and recite:

It's cocoa and animals that I love the most!

No one is talking and I do not know if anyone is looking at me. I cannot look up to find out, however. I cannot stop. Now the snack.

The yogurt is smoother and easier to swallow. I keep reciting nonetheless.

Chew. Swallow. One more spoonful. Think of the next line, the girls, the morning walk. Just a bit more. Breathe. Good, now only the animal crackers are left.

I line them up as I used to and contemplate their childish shapes. Maman, I am twenty-six years old and scared of little animals.

But I eat one, then the other, and recite the last stanza. I finish the poem and the snack at the same time.

And it is 10:30. The table is cleared in front of me. The room, and my brain, are quiet.

24

I am not dead. I am drained but not dead. So drained I can barely walk. Perhaps it is a good thing. I cannot think of what I just made myself do.

None of the girls speak to me. That is good too; I do not trust myself to talk just now. Now I need to be alone and to cry. I need to process this meal. This meal that stood against everything my brain has firmly believed for so many years. I need time for the yogurt, bagel, cream cheese, crackers, and anxiety to settle down.

I'd like to use the bathroom please,
but am not given that luxury:
You can go after group therapy, Anna. Now follow the other girls, please.

I have no choice. I follow the others to the back of the house, a sunroom, for my first group session at 17 Swann Street. There are chairs set in a circle in the middle.

Each girl automatically takes a seat. Here too, each has her spot. I hesitate: *Where is mine?* Three voices call out at once:
This seat is free if you like.
They have spoken to me!

Emm was right: *No grudges here.* I sink into the nearest chair gratefully. I notice her looking at me, a few chairs away. *Thank you,* I mouth. She nods.

Valerie, across from me, is obviously still shaken from both the breakfast incident and her last snack, but her fingers are unclenched and she even, maybe, I imagine, smiles at me.

Julia is sitting to my right, headphones around her neck now. She shakes my hand buoyantly:

Ah, the French rebel. Glad to meet you, neighbor! I'm Julia, from Bedroom 4.

Hello Julia, I'm sorry I got you into trouble at breakfast—

but she brushes it off:

Nah, don't be sorry! No worries, I was just trying my luck anyway. They won't slap my wrists too hard for stealing a few packets of sweetener.

Speaking of wrists, my osteopenic bones are cracking in her jovial grip. I look down and see fresh calluses on her knuckles: *Russell's sign,* caused by self-induced vomiting. The skin is chafed where it scraped against her teeth while she was making herself gag. I do not want to imagine what the inside of her mouth must look like.

There are dark circles under her eyes, but she seems quite upbeat.

It's the coffee, it's still morning,

she answers my unvoiced question with a wink.

The days are all right. I like the meals here, and I chew gum during sessions. It's the nights that are hard. But hey, we share a wall. Let me know if my music is too loud.

Bulimia nervosa. Julia does not look emaciated or frail. She is warm and misleadingly jolly, but, as she said, it is still morning.

She pops a piece of chewing gum in her mouth. It must be allowed here.

Want some? I'm always well stocked.

No thank you,

but good to know. I used to chew gum all the time as well, to keep hunger and anxiety at bay.

I look away from Julia as a therapist walks in. I have not seen this lady before: loud bleached hair, loud bleached smile. She sits in the last empty seat, closing the circle of quiet patients, and, queuing all the loud bleached sympathy she has, asks:

How is everyone today?

She receives no response, though in our defense, I do not know what she expects to hear. The question seems far too high-pitched to be anything but rhetorical. It clashes as loudly as her hair against the melancholy in the room. Everyone around me seems too tired for theater. Except for Julia, who pops a bubble.

Emm finally breaks the silence, on everyone's grateful behalf:

Everyone's fine.

Fueled by the answer, any answer, the smile beams louder. The white teeth are unnaturally straight. The therapist turns to look at me specifically:

How are you today?

Well, I am on the spot, unprepared, and extremely uncomfortable. I just had a terrifying meal. My stomach hurts and I want to cry, but I doubt that is what she wants to hear.

Fortunately, I do not have to reply. She speaks again instead:

Welcome to group therapy. These sessions are a safe space where you can share and receive feedback.

I nod politely and whisper *thank you,* hopefully loud enough that she hears. I then look down at my pink trainers, signaling she can move on.

She does not.

Since this is your first time with us, would you like to introduce yourself and tell us a little bit about your past?

Oh I most certainly would not, but as I am coming to learn, at 17 Swann Street most questions are really instructions in sweetened, buttered disguise.

I could introduce myself—

Hello, my name is Anna.

—but my past is not hers to know. As far as she is concerned, I am just another patient at an eating-disorder treatment center. My disease is just a variation of that of every other girl in this room. All of whom, I suspect, have heard more than their share of sad anorexia stories.

That's all.

The therapist's eyes widen, glance briefly at the clock, then look back at me with a clear message: I am going to stop wasting her time and share. I look back at my feet, wondering how and where to begin. *Help . . .*

It comes from the girls. Valerie, to my surprise, goes first:

Where did you grow up? Any siblings? Pets?

Another patient chimes in:

Married? Kids? What do you do in real life?

Emm asks me why I came to the States. Julia wants to know if I like jazz. Another patient— potatoes in small bites, I remember, from dinner last night—asks with a sly smile:

Will the gorgeous man who came to see you yesterday be back?

The irritated therapist tries to redirect the conversation onto a therapeutic track:

Or, if you would rather, you could tell us about how your eating disorder developed.

I would rather not. So I turn to the questions the other girls asked.

I grew up in Paris. I have a sister and a brother, I tell Valerie first.

I am the eldest. My sister and I are very different

but very close. She is the sophisticated banker; vodka martinis and the like. My brother . . .

was hit by a car when he was seven. His name is Camil. But I do not want to mention him, or Maman.

I switch tracks, hoping no one notices:

I do have a pet: a limping dog called Leopold. He lives in Paris with my father.

If they did notice, no one mentions it. I am grateful to the girls yet again.

Yes I am married. To the gorgeous man from yesterday,

I add for potatoes-in-small-bites' sake.

His name is Matthias. He is kind and my best friend and we have been married for three years.

Space, and then,

No kids.

Now, what do I do in real life? *I cannot remember,* is the honest answer. I have not had a real life in years. This one I have been spending mostly just stopping myself from eating. It takes up a lot of my time. And energy, and concentration. My brain is slow and rarely looks beyond anticipating the next hunger pangs. Or back past the guilt of the last bite. By nighttime, it is exhausted. I sleep.

In real life I starve and I sleep, but I know that is not a proper answer for this crowd. So I rummage through my memories to pre-anorexia:

I was a dancer for a while. I was not very good. I also hurt my knee, then we moved here, and
now I remember:

Now I work as a cashier at a supermarket. Or I used to before checking in here. I hated it. It was supposed to be temporary, but at least it paid a salary.

I trail off with the thought.

In an ideal world, I would go to university. I went straight to ballet after school. I think I would study art history, or Italian, or maybe teach dance to children. . . .

I realize no one had asked me about that. Embarrassed, I move on.

To Emm:

Matthias was offered a position at a research laboratory here. He is a physicist and very smart. Or I am biased. I don't know.

The offer was generous, and we were struggling in Paris, especially when I stopped dancing.

It was a brilliant opportunity for Matthias,
and we needed the money.

And now I need a lighter interlude. Julia's question provides it:

I do not know enough about jazz, but what I do know I love. I love music that moves me. The saxophone. I like Billie Holiday.

I wrap up:

And yes, Matthias is coming tonight!
and add to myself, self-consciously: *I hope I*

can put some makeup and perfume on before he arrives.

That leaves the therapist's question unanswered. I hope she does not notice.

She does:

So what made you seek treatment for your eating disorder?

Seek treatment for my eating disorder, like a case in a medical textbook. The question is as cold and indifferent as everything behind that façade.

I think of every possible answer I can give the overzealous therapist. I open my mouth, ready to fire sarcasm, but to my surprise the truth comes out:

I am here because Matthias and I went home to Paris last Christmas. I had not seen my family in three years. My father was waiting at the airport. He did not recognize me at first, and when he did he cried.

He did not hug me either, too scared that if he did something in me would break.

It was supposed to be a happy occasion. My father, my sister, we were all there. But I could not eat, was too cold to go outside. They were so frightened, they confronted me. They begged me to get help. We fought and I left angry.

It was extremely sad.

Back then I decided it was none of their business, and I made that very clear. If I wanted

116

to die it was my choice. They were not around, and neither was Matthias. No right to interfere.

I wince, remembering the harsh words I said, the phone calls I stopped answering.

We returned to Saint Louis and Matthias returned to work. Then everything unraveled. So quickly.

I realize I am speaking too much and too intimately again. I falter, but cannot retreat now; they are all waiting, even the therapist, plastic smile folded away.

I try to bring the story to a clean close:

Nothing dramatic happened. I just fainted in the bathroom one night. And a few other times. Matthias found me.

And when I woke up he was crying.

I did not have a choice. I knew I was hurting him—

but I had never made him cry before.

So I came here.

I turn to the therapist.

And that's it. May I use the bathroom now please?

25

It was the end of the world.

It was not, she told herself again. It only felt like it. Just the end of a world. Just a job as a cashier, to help pay the bills.

She was still Anna. She was still a dancer. She still loved poetry and sparkling wine, but Matthias worked long hours that felt even longer in this city where she was alone. Her super--market shifts would fill the time perfectly, she reasoned in her uniform.

She was where she needed to be. Missing home was a tangent. She would go back for Christmas, or in the spring. Her shifts would help them save for the trip too, and buy presents for her family.

So she helped elderly men count quarters, pennies, dimes to pay for their two slices of ham and bread. She helped ladies with polished nails and Chanel handbags navigate coupons and food stamps, ashamed.

She avoided eye contact with the smug smiles and fake IDs that bought too much alcohol on Friday nights. She made small talk with the weekly Sunday evening purchase of seven frozen chicken pennes with mushroom sauce, for one.

She saw downcast eyes and furtive wads of cash pay for the morning-after pill. Bags of perishable pastries, cheese, and meat get thrown out every night. Gloved hands that dropped nickels at her feet and did not bother to pick them up, blue and chapped ones that begged for them outside. That would not have minded stale pastries.

And at the bus stop one night she saw a homeless man under the bench, frozen or starved to death. She could not eat or sleep that night.

Not the end of the world, just the end of a world, she tried to think as she cried. That night did end. Spring came and went, and they did not go to Paris.

She tried to remember the Sorbonne, the cafés, the hidden nooks in libraries where they had spent hours kissing, reading Verlaine, Camus, Stendhal, Sagan, Pushkin. Instead, she saw the dead man at the bus stop and the overflowing shopping carts. The gluttony, the starvation, the disparity in between. It was just the end of a world.

26

How is your mood this morning?

I roll my eyes.

After group therapy, Direct Care had rushed me from my bathroom break to the psychiatrist's office.

Why I need a psychiatrist is beyond me. My mood is as fine as it could be, under the present circumstances.

Fine, thank you. How is yours?

The short portly man perched high on his chair peers at me from above his glasses. He does not appreciate my humor, I gather.

How would you describe your mood in general?

Happy.

Ecstatic, elated, thrilled.

The nurse says you woke up quite early this morning.

At five actually.

Yes.

Do you always?

Yes.

Why?

Because anxiety rises early.

Because it is calm in the mornings.
Do you have a history of insomnia?
No.
Mental illness?
No.
Besêes not being able to eat.
Depression, anxiety, hopelessness?
No need to be dramatic.
Do you drink?
Moderately.
Do you smoke?
No.
Other forms of substance abuse?
No.
Compulsive exercise?
I choose not to answer. He writes *compulsive exercise* down.
Do you have any trauma in your past?
My first response is:
No.
No, my family played board games and went on picnics on Sundays. Hikes when it was sunny, the museum when it rained. We loved to travel when we could, and when we could not, we had piles and piles of books to read and other adventures to go on.
No history of trauma at all?
A box in my bedroom upstairs. Camil's drawings, his little white bear. I was the shoelace-tier, crêpe-flipper, finder of his missing gloves.

Self-proclaimed protector who failed to protect him from that speeding car.

My history is one of summer figs in Toulouse and presents on Christmas mornings. Until we lost Camil somewhere in there and everything fell apart. Sophie would not speak of him. Neither would Papa. And one afternoon, locked in the bathroom, Maman chose to join her son.

But that is all in a box I placed under my bed in the Van Gogh room. I look straight at the psychiatrist and answer his question:

No.

Do you have any thoughts of harming others or yourself?

Trick question; I remember the form. I know I could lose all my rights *if the institution or Matthias believe I am not of sound mind.*

So I smile placidly at the psychiatrist, as I will as long as I am here, and give him the right answer:

No, I am fine. Thank you very much for your time.

27

Sacher torte! Sacher torte!

The audience's demands were clear. Sacher torte it would be for dessert. Of course: it was Anna's specialty.

Why have I never heard about this famous dessert of yours?

Matthias asked, lover of chocolate himself.

Anna turned deep red.

I forgot.

She honestly had.

The recipe for Sacher torte and memory of her making it had been misplaced, along with many other things, somewhere in her anorexic mind sometime over the hazy past few years. Like names, addresses, faces she used to know. Entire hours, days, months of her life. Like mornings that began without an alarm clock, uninterrupted nights. A closet once full of summer dresses that she could actually wear. Winters that were not so painfully cold, summer days that were truly warm. Like the taste of dark chocolate, rich espresso, and brandy infused in the Sacher torte.

It was all for the best, she would think when-

ever she noticed she was forgetting. What she could not remember, she would not miss.

But now she needed the recipe. It had to be here somewhere. She found it on the back of a black-and-white postcard in one of Maman's cookbooks.

Had it really contained so many eggs? She cut the number in half. The butter and dark chocolate too . . . Actually, she would skip the butter and swap the sugar with sweetener.

She used to make whipped cream to top the Sacher torte, but it was so uselessly unhealthy. . . .

And Anna! Don't forget the whipped cream!

Fine, she would make whipped cream. On the side.

While she bustled about the little cubicle that was a Parisian version of a kitchen, her father, husband, and sister were whispering in the other room:

We cannot go to the Christmas market! She'll freeze! Have you seen how many layers she already has on in here?

But we always go, and to midnight mass.

Well, this year we will not,

Sophie snapped.

I also think we should limit our outings in general in the evenings. Forget the restaurants, we can eat at home. She will be more comfortable here.

That reminds me, I need to slip out before the last superette closes to buy more apples, otherwise there will be nothing she can eat.

What about a baguette?

Have you seen her eat bread yet?

Matthias, has she been eating bread?

Matthias had no idea. He had not seen her eating anything lately.

Someone's stomach grumbled. All their stomachs grumbled.

I am hungry. Aren't you?

I am starving,

said Sophie,

but it is so hard to eat around her! She makes me feel like a pig! She had broth and lettuce for lunch—

I thought she had some of your lentil stew,

Matthias countered, a little defensively,

and the fruit salad with coulis for dessert.

Pay attention, Matthias. She only took some soup too, because she was trying to please me. She dumped it in the sink while we were talking, and when she saw the coulis, she said she didn't feel like fruit salad and had an apple instead.

Sophie was still whispering, but pointedly.

Papa, you should get the apples before the superette closes.

She looked at Matthias hopefully:

And maybe a few pears and bananas?

He shook his head.

Just apples then. Oh, and Papa, make sure you get coffee too.

How can we have run out already?

No one answered. Anna's voice called out from the kitchen:

Could someone come and take a look at this please? Something went wrong with the recipe.

28

I hate doctors.

All doctors?

Yes, all. And nutritionists too.

Matthias and I are out on the porch. The weather is pleasant this evening. I am not; day two had been painful and heavy. And dinner had been worse.

I deduce that you had your first meetings with your team.

Wry smile, barely concealed. I resent his light-hearted response, but

Yes, and my first session of group therapy.

How did they go?

Not well.

Not that I really know how they should; I had never met with a therapist, psychiatrist, or nutritionist before.

They treat me like a child, Matthias! Like a patient at a mental institution.

The words *not of sound mind* replay in my head.

You are a patient, Anna.

Yes, but I am not stupid or crazy. I chose to come here. You should have heard the

condescension in their voices, telling me what to eat and what to think!

It's their job. They are just trying to help. You are sick—

I am not sick! I have a problem.

You have a disease that is killing you.

I want to keep my voice low but feel it rising with my irritation. My spine tenses. I fire:

Don't be dramatic!

Matthias's face darkens at my snap. He waits for me to finish my tirade, knowing there is more to come.

I said I have a problem! And I am fixing it! I am going to fix it. I just . . .

but my voice quivers, and my throat feels tight. *I just . . .* struggle with the rest of that sentence.

I end lamely:

It's just hard.

No, it is exhausting. Today was exhausting. The meals, sessions with the girls and my team. How had things gotten to this? How had everything gotten so difficult?

How does one forget how to eat? How does one forget how to breathe? Worse: how does one remember? And how does happiness feel?

I sink back into the wicker chair. Matthias puts his hand on mine. No, I do not need the pity. I sit back up before the tears come.

Don't worry, I will fix this,

I tell Matthias.

I will figure it out. I can do this on my own, I do not need—

But Matthias interrupts:

No.

Silence. What side is he on?

No you cannot do this on your own. You tried, remember, Anna? You promised me you would eat, and your father and family,

The confrontation, the hours of begging, defending, arguing in the living room on Christmas Day. The promises I had made to make them stop crying, stop worrying about me.

and it did not work.

I tried!

I protest.

I am still trying, all right? I am doing my best!

But I am the only one shouting. Matthias takes my hand again.

Softly:

Anna, you weigh eighty-eight pounds.

My throat is tight again. I do not trust my voice to reply, am too tired to withdraw my hand. The tears are flowing, treacherous and unauthorized, freely down my face.

I finally let him put his arms around me, crying quietly into his shirt.

I know you tried, Anna. I know you really did, but if you could have fixed this you would have. If this were "just" a problem you and I would not be sitting here.

29

Finally back at the—gloriously, miraculously—empty flat. The Métro had stopped, twice, to their immense frustration. Interruptions sur la ligne quatre. *The run up the six flights of stairs had also been interrupted by steamy, breathless kissing stops, Anna's back against the cold wall, Matthias's fingers tangled in her hair.*

Now they were alone. No friends, no flatmates, very little furniture left in the bedroom. Matthias's suitcase was already closed and set outside by its door. They slammed against it. Neither of them noticed. The floorboards cracked under their hurried feet. A trail of discarded black heels, fine black tights, and brown leather Oxfords. Bare feet.

Her cold fingers fumbled with the buttons of his shirt, numb and in a hurry and clumsy. His hands were icy on her back. She shivered but pulled him closer.

Black dress to the floor, then the black satin lingerie. They tumbled onto the old mattress. It barely squeaked under their weight; by now it had memorized their shape.

She claimed the ridge over his collarbone and

the freckle she knew was at its end. He drew the line down her spine and circled to the tip of her hip bone. No clothes, no curtains, but abundant moonlight flooding the chambre de bonne. *No covers, no need. Time in suspension, they fell into waves of silence and heat.*

Later, much later, his arms around her. Her face in his chest, breathing quietly at his heart. They fell asleep naked. They always had, leg over leg, skin on skin.

The next morning, the windows were foggy. Cold water splashed on cold faces. A nearly forgotten toothbrush and sweater stuffed hurriedly into the suitcase. Maneuvering around the treacherous floorboards, they tried to tiptoe out quietly; their flatmates were back and still asleep behind their closed bedroom doors.

The suitcase down the six winding flights of the narrow stairwell was an adventure. They dragged it together to the station and onto the RER.

Finally on their way to the airport they finally kissed.

Bonjour.
Bonjour,
she smiled.

30

Day three in the peach-pink house shaded by a magnolia tree. White wicker furniture on the front porch, hydrangeas growing at the back. Emm stands in the sun, at the beginning of the tiny well-trodden path that takes the girls at 17 Swann Street on the same morning walk every day.

Except today I am joining her, and Julia, and Direct Care. And Chloe, who has kids, I learned this morning, and Katerina, Matthias's fan. Valerie does not join us, nor does the seventh girl, whose name I still do not know. She does not speak much and does not seem to like walks. I wonder how long she has been here.

At this point I have mastered the routine that begins with vitals and weights and develops into shower, coffee, and the daily word jumbles with breakfast. I find my footing and comfort, somewhat, in this constant repetition. All other aspects of life here are volatile; at least the routine is safe.

We begin walking. Emm informs me that the itinerary does not change. Right after the second red door. Left, left, right. Turn back at the roundabout with white and blue hydrangeas. Left, right, right, left.

We go on the walk in two straight lines. What an odd group we must seem. Vapory girls in loose T-shirts floating behind Direct Care and Emm in turquoise. We cross a number of people on their own safe morning routines: the retired, full-time front-porch newspaper reader, the stroller-pushing yoga mom, the dog walker listening to music, the old couple holding hands, walking slow. All greet us, none stare; they must know about the girls at 17 Swann Street.

There are children at the house on the second corner playing outside on the lawn. They say *good morning,* so well-behaved, as we pass them by. The birds and squirrels are out and about too, and a humming gardener. Toward the end we pass a Saint Bernard. Emm tells me his name is Gerald.

All too soon we are back from fresh air and blue sky to a whole day we will spend indoors, but another dependable constant emerges: at ten to ten, the mailman.

As he did yesterday, he takes our outgoing mail and hands us letters, postcards, and parcels, bits of the world that the world has sent to us.

Every day but Sunday,
he says.

At ten o'clock, we have midmorning snack, but the mail makes it palatable. Every day but

Sunday, we share whatever good news and goodies we receive.

Then two hours in session, not always group therapy. Sometimes nutrition, psychology, coping skills. At different times, each of us will be called away to meet with the members of our team.

At twelve thirty we will receive the signal to stand up and form two straight lines. In those we will walk to the yellow house next door for a game of Russian roulette: Lunch.

Someone, at some point, will get hurt and cry, but at least Rita will be there: the Italian-American cook who serves all her love and gossip with the food. And no matter what or how difficult lunch is, we will tell Rita it was good. She will beam, and for better or worse, it will end at one fifteen.

On Monday and Friday afternoons, we have yoga to look forward to. On Tuesdays, as Valerie's letter said, we all have the cottage cheese. On Wednesdays, we have art class with Lucy. Dance again with her on Saturdays. Dance! On Sundays, music lessons after lunch. And apple cinnamon tea after meals. And I, the luckiest girl in this house, have a date with Matthias every evening.

Each patient gets a room, a journal, a cubby, and a water bottle to her name. And in community space, her own seat. I choose an old battered armchair.

Back from my first walk, I sink into it, calm. Valerie is writing in her spot. Emm, in hers, is knitting. *Is she really knitting?* The quiet girl is asleep.

Julia, next to me, is deeply engrossed in the last word jumble of the day. I am stuck on that one too. I stare at it with her.

Just then Direct Care walks in with a patient we have not seen before. She seems cold and exhausted, leaning almost entirely on Direct Care for support.

We make room for her on the couch. She lies down, wrapped in a thick woolen blanket I immediately associate with the inside of an ambulance. Curled into a ball, she closes her eyes. Without a word, Direct Care walks out.

The other girls, unfazed, return to their knitting, writing, napping, jumbles. I make to leave my armchair to welcome the new patient, but Julia touches my arm:

Not this one.

Not this one. Why not?

We call patients like that weekenders.

What patients like that?

What are weekenders?

Wry, sad smile. Jumbles aside. Julia leans in toward me. I do the same. She whispers:

Weekenders are patients who usually leave before you even realize they're here. Involuntary admissions, most of them, and they tend to make that very clear. They're either sad, angry, or sleeping on the couch. Behold Exhibit A.

Her dispassionate description suits the unnamed, shivering girl.

I try to stay away from them. Not a very lively bunch. Very, very sick girls.

Why do they leave so quickly then?

Because they are too sick to be here. They need to be hospitalized. Too thin, too sad, too many medical complications. Too far away in their heads.

How horrible.

You'll see what I mean when this one wakes up. She'll stare out the window for hours.

I do not like the term "this one." I wish I knew the girl's name.

Why are such patients brought here at all then?

Julia shrugs.

Wishful thinking mostly. I guess their families don't realize how serious the situation is. Or want to.

She reflects further:

Sometimes they come here because insurance has not approved higher care. Sometimes it has, but there are no beds available in hospital psych wards. But if that's the case, one should free up by tomorrow and the new girl will be transferred.

How do you know a bed will free up?

Someone is bound to die or be discharged,

comes the simple, callous reply.

How smoothly she had said it! I withdraw, appalled. Julia notices but does not take offense. She smiles sadly at my indignation and speaks again, this time softer:

Look, Anna, and look around you. Every patient is a tragedy here. It sucks, I know, but there are too many of us for me to cry over every one.

I understand. Julia is not jaded, just trying to protect herself. Choosing wisely where to invest her heart. She forces a smile and jokes:

Heck, if I should cry over someone, I would probably start with myself!

I do not laugh, but I lean back toward her. We are both quiet for a moment. When she speaks again she is not joking:

Actually, I would start with Emm.

Emm?

How come?

Because Emm is at the other end of the spectrum.

Across from us, we watch her knit.

Emm and 17 Swann Street go way back,

Julia says in a lower voice.

Yes, I remember: four years back. Julia continues:

She's a regular. Knows this place by heart: the schedule, the rules, the rooms with the best view, the weekly menus, all the staff—they're her friends.

Is that bad?

140

You tell me, hon. Is it bad that she knows that the smoothies are actually made from a powdered mix? Or which nurse will slip you antacids or, if you ask really nicely, sleeping pills?

I see where Julia is going with this.

Emm has been at 17 Swann so long it's become part of her. Patients like her, the regulars, they . . . They get comfortable here.

That makes terrifying sense.

Four years at 17 Swann Street, in any place, and that place becomes home. Staff becomes family. Treatment becomes familiar. The schedule, even the menus become safe.

Most regulars never get discharged, and those who do know they will be back.

I nod. The real world is fraught with unrewarding jobs and hurtful relationships. Bills to be paid every month, food to be consumed every day. At least here in treatment the cook makes the meals and staff takes care of the dishes. Insurance pays rent and somebody else changes the lightbulbs and mows the lawn. The real world is lonely but here doctors have pills and therapists always have time to listen. I cannot believe I do, but in a way, I understand Emm.

Emm is still knitting. The movement is predictable, the pattern repeats itself. This is not real life, but perhaps she has no interest in pursuing one. Perhaps all-inclusive survival on this side of the walls is enough.

141

As for you,
Julia interrupts my thoughts,
you're a different kind of patient. I think you're one of the lucky ones.
Which ones?
The ones here for someone else.
Someone else, outside here, waiting for me at 45 Furstenberg Street.
You have a reason to survive,
Julia says casually as she reaches for her pouch and begins rummaging through it for gum.
See, Emm's life is here, not outside these walls. And the girl on the couch doesn't want one. You, with a little help and a little food in your belly . . . Dammit, I'm out of gum.
A reason to survive.
Never mind! False alarm!
She pops two pieces in her mouth at the same time and offers me one.
I shake my head slowly.
No, but thank you, Julia.
Silence for a moment, then I dare:
What about you?
What about me?
Pop.
What kind of patient are you?
She does not answer. I do not ask again.

31

The day is over, as is dinner, whatever dinner was. It is 7:20. I rush to my room, brush my teeth and my hair, dab a little bit of blush on my cheeks, one, two spritzes of perfume, then scramble down the stairs just as Matthias's blue car pulls into the driveway.

He steps out of the car at 7:28, rings the doorbell at 7:30. It marks the beginning of the countdown: we have ninety precious minutes left.

He is well dressed and smells nice. I know that scent: tobacco musk. He knows mine: apple and jasmine. He kisses me at the door. Toothpaste.

I ask Direct Care for permission to sit outside with my husband. Permission laughingly granted,

So long as he has you back inside by evening snack!

I ask about his day. He says work was fine, and that our little orchid back home is as well. He declares being quite concerned, however, that it has not bloomed since last year. I try not to smile, but

I can see your mouth twitching, Anna, but you cannot imagine how worried I've been! I blame you for this, you know, buying us an orchid and then running off to treatment. Do you know what kind of maintenance orchids need?

Would you have preferred a cactus?

A cactus! Yes, a cactus! You have to be purpose-ful about letting a cactus die. When all this is over, I'll buy you a cactus.

Haha! You have a deal.

He asks me about my day. I keep my account just as light. I tell him about a book I have been reading. I found it in community space.

Rilke. His poetry is magical. It transports me away from here.

Do you have time to read?

I do in the morning, after vitals and weights and before breakfast at eight. I love it. It is quiet and the sun rises and the Van Gogh room just lights up.

You always did like mornings best.

I did. I do.

Oh! Did I tell you? I went on the walk this morning.

How was it?

Too short, but freeing.

Are you making friends?

I laugh.

I am trying. Most keep to themselves, and we are all quite busy anyway.

144

Busy? What, with all the meals?

Once again, it strikes me how little Matthias, or any normal person, can understand. How little of an eating disorder the naked eye can actually see. Busy?

Yes busy,

to the point of exhaustion. Every bite and every thought is. But to anyone else, perhaps we just look like girls with bad eating habits.

Six times a day, Matthias.

And you're doing it! I am proud of you, Anna. Don't stop.

He beams, and I am suddenly gripped by fear: *What if I do stop?*

What if I let you down, Matthias?

I do not voice that thought. Instead:

This afternoon, I chose my cereal for tomorrow's breakfast.

I try to keep my voice casual and fail. He hears it and takes my hand. No longer lighthearted, Matthias says:

You are the bravest girl in the world.

He does understand. He does hear the constant screaming in my head. But he will not give me pity, so he asks:

Did you pick the Frosted Flakes?

Taken aback, I answer shortly:

No, Matthias. Plain Cheerios.

How could you possibly pick the Cheerios? We both know they taste like cardboard!

The Frosties, on the other hand, are grrreat!

And his favorite. And, incidentally, covered with glistening, frightening sugar crystals.

I happen to like Cheerios,

I object, my feathers ruffled the wrong way.

But Matthias calls my bluff:

No you don't. You like Frosties. Or at least you used to, and Lucky Charms.

Not at all!

I protest, my claws out in defense of my anorexic lie. I ready myself to counter with arguments of food coloring and high sugar content . . . but Matthias speaks before me:

The bottom line is that Frosties are endorsed by Tony the Tiger.

I cannot believe my ears.

So?

So tiger trumps bee, obviously. When in doubt, pick the cereal endorsed by the tiger. That's Frosties. I rest my case.

I laugh, genuinely, at my husband's unconventional approach to therapy: *Pick the Frosties. Do not be afraid. Tiger trumps bee and anorexia. Simple.*

If only it were, if only it could be. If only I could believe it.

Tonight, though, I want to. It is such a beautiful evening out here. Matthias looks handsome. He smells nice. He loves me. He is smiling mischievously.

So I let myself play along, if only for an evening. *All right, Matthias,*
Next time I will pick the Frosties,
because a talking tiger said so.

32

She was going to die.

What do you mean: "The machine is out of order"?

It was 7:00 P.M. on Wednesday. They were at the movies. Matthias and Anna went to the movies on Wednesday nights. Anna began fasting on Wednesday mornings—Tuesday nights she ate an apple, perhaps—so that by 7:00 P.M. on Wednesday her brain would allow her to have the popcorn. Small.

Anna had movie theater popcorn once a week, on Wednesdays. She compensated for the oil by skipping breakfast and running for ten extra minutes on Thursdays. But that particular Wednesday it was 7:00 P.M. and they had bought their tickets, but the popcorn machine was out of order and she was going to die.

May I offer you any other concessions? Anything else at all?

She had long passed hunger and was nauseated with starvation. Her eyes blurred as she looked at the display.

A pretzel? Impossible.

Candy? Had the world gone mad?

Nachos? She could not accurately estimate their calorie content.

No, he could not offer her anything else, because there was nothing else that she could eat.

It is all right,
said Matthias,
we can eat when we get home,
steering her away from the concession stand.

No they could not, she almost screamed. Home was a two-hour movie and drive away from here. She would be dead by then.

33

Evening snack is interrupted by the sound of a siren and the flashing lights of an ambulance streaming in through the windows.

Direct Care does not look surprised; she glances at her watch and nods. She stands up and says:

Ladies, I'm going to leave you for a few minutes. I trust—

But she actually does not, she realizes. She calls to the nurse's station:

Mary?

Mary watches us sternly while Direct Care goes to the front door.

Men in gray jumpsuits wheel a stretcher in. I notice the doors are wide enough. It takes less than a minute: the weekender and her blanket are lifted from the couch. Onto the stretcher and rolled away. The sirens and lights fade out. Julia had been right: she had not left the couch. And we had not learned her name.

I feel sick. I turn to Julia for help. She just shrugs. She told me so. The rest of the girls, even Valerie, keep eating, looking straight down at their bowls.

Later, much later, I cannot sleep, thinking of the bed that freed up in the psych ward of a hospital somewhere today. Julia cannot sleep either; I can hear her music through our wall. And her footsteps, pacing, pounding in rhythm.

Julia only acts nonchalant.

She had gone through two full packs of gum, then upstairs after her snack. I had followed shortly after to escape the macabre mood in community space.

Now, hours later, the house is quiet, except for Julia's music. And she is crying. Perhaps she feels lonely, scared, trapped, sad, in pain. Perhaps she feels sorry for the weekender, perhaps she feels sorry for herself. I knock on our wall:

Hey.

Silence. Then:

Hey.

No need to say any more.

I hate the night. The dark, ironically, makes many things far too clear. I hate empty beds, in treatment centers, psych wards. Matthias in ours alone.

I cannot sleep as I wonder how long Matthias will keep coming back. How many visiting hours it will take before he grows tired and stops. If he does, will I blame him? Will I be able to let him go? Do I love him enough? I love him more than anything.

Then what will happen to me?

Julia had called girls like me lucky, because they *have a reason to survive.* On the other side of the wall, she plays Billie Holiday, in my honor.

34

Thursday morning. 11:00 A.M. Something different is happening. Instead of a therapist, the nutritionist walks in the sunroom, announcing:

Weekly meal planning,

to which the room responds with a general groan.

Indifferent, she sets three stacks of forms on the floor. The patients seem to know what to do; they stand in line, each girl takes one set from each pile and returns to her seat.

I go last and then, forms in hand, look awkwardly around for help. The nutritionist ignores me studiously, examining the polish on her nails.

On Thursdays we get to choose all our meals for the coming week, Monday to Sunday.

Emm. She pulls her seat closer to mine. I could hug her. I do not dare.

Professional as ever, she hands me a pen before I even ask for one. She has two, just in case. Of course she does.

All right, you should have three sets of seven: breakfast, lunch, and dinner. Good. We have twenty minutes to fill them out. Let's start with the easy ones: breakfast.

I look at the first page: *Breakfast 1—Monday.*
Two options:
Circle A or B.
The choices are straightforward enough:
Frosties or Cheerios on Monday?
Plain oatmeal or cinnamon on Wednesday?
Vanilla yogurt or strawberry?
Not circling either is also a choice,
says Emm.
Liquid nutritional substitute.
Even the dense, high-calorie supplement is offered in a choice of three flavors:
Vanilla, Chocolate, Pecan
Emm and I fill out the breakfast forms rapidly. Lunch and dinner prove more complicated.

Every lunch and dinner menu comprises three courses: an appetizer, a main dish, and a dessert. Two options are offered for each.
Again, circle A or B,
and Emm begins to fill hers. But I lag behind, frozen at the starting line: the very first appetizer on Monday.
Caesar salad with dressing and Parmesan cheese
OR
Basket of French fries
Parmesan cheese? Caesar dressing? *French fries?*
I skip the appetizer for now.
Perhaps the main course . . .

Fish fillet
OR
Mac and cheese
I am about to cry.
I know they look scary. Don't let them over-whelm you. Let's start with the first one,
Emm says.
I am so grateful. I look at her shakily:
You do not have to do this.
I know.
Her poker face is replaced with a smile. For a second.
Didn't Valerie tell you the rules? It's what we do.
Then she snaps back to business and the menu:
Caesar salad or fries?
Salad, I suppose, but before I circle it, Emm says:
A few rules first.
Number one: know yourself. I know the salad seems a safer choice, but if you aren't willing to down a gallon of mayonnaise and eat every bit of cheese, then stick to the French fries.
I hesitate. Then circle the fries.
Next, the main course:
Be clear about your priorities, Anna: if you circle the fish, you must eat it. How committed are you to being a vegetarian? If you are, tough luck: mac and cheese.
But the cream! The cheese . . .

My voice gets caught in my throat. I am panicky, but Emm is firm:

Priorities.

Swallowing my tears, I circle the mac and cheese.

Now dessert:

Yogurt and granola

OR

Chocolate milkshake

What the hell, I have come this far. Chocolate milkshake it is.

Rule number three: don't be a hero,

says Emm. I look at her, confused. She raises an eyebrow at me:

If you could really eat fries, mac and cheese, and a chocolate milkshake in one meal, you would not be in a treatment center, would you? Don't bite off more than you can chew.

Literally.

One challenge at a time. Start with the fries. Next week, conquer the shake. Be kind to yourself; you have six meals a day and seven days of those to complete.

Six meals a day for seven days. I am exhausted after just the first lunch. But Emm nudges me forward and we make our way through them.

One circled option at a time. Other insight:

Be realistic. There is no "lighter" option in a place like this. The meals are planned and portioned so that all options are calorically equivalent. Everything will be scary and large. Everything will make you gain weight. So green beans or ice cream, choose what you are most likely to swallow, and maybe enjoy?

Which brings us to rule number five:

Use the resources you have, like the schedule. No high-volume lunch on oatmeal breakfast day. No saucy dishes before yoga; you do not want to have acid reflux in your downward-facing dog.

She then shares the biggest secret of all:

And if you really hit a wall, you can always strike the whole lunch or dinner out and opt for a sub meal.

A sub meal! That's right! We have, at all times, three substitute meal options to choose from:

SUBSTITUTE MEAL A:

A ham and cheese sandwich, with pretzels, and yogurt and fruit.

SUBSTITUTE MEAL B:

A peanut butter and jelly sandwich, with pretzels, and yogurt and fruit.

And Sub Meal C, I discover, is what I was served for my first meal here:

A whole-wheat bagel with hummus, carrots, and yogurt and fruit.

You only get seven sub meals a week, though, so use them wisely,

Emm warns. But I am not listening, holding on to Sub Meal C with my sanity.

It had been a paralyzing first meal. A terrifying, cataclysmic experience. It had seemed impossible. It had not been. Now it seems like a dream.

The vegetarian option for lunch on Tuesday is a black bean burger. Sub Meal C.

For dinner: a cheesy baked potato, topped with sour cream. Sub Meal C. On to Wednesday, where the nonmeat option is a tomato basil flatbread. I could swallow that. Dinner, however, is spaghetti marinara. Cue my third Sub Meal C.

By the time I reach lunch on Friday, however, I have run out of sub meals.

Reevaluate your choices. This is not sustainable,

says Emm.

Why not? I protest.

The voice in my head argues desperately: *Sub Meal C is a well-balanced meal!* It contains fat, carbohydrates, vegetables, and protein. Reliably familiar and bland. If the purpose of food is nutrition for survival then I can just survive on that!

There! I have cured my anorexia on my fourth day at 17 Swann Street. But even I know it cannot be this simple. I turn to Emm for help. *Emm?*

But Emm is circling her own menu options, deliberately leaving me on my own. The rules are clear: *Only seven sub meals.* I try not to panic.

Most of the other girls have already finished and submitted their forms. The rest are nearly done. I look at the clock: I have four minutes left.

Animal crackers and cocoa to drink. If they can do this I can. I flip back to Tuesday's menu and circle the black bean burger for lunch. I skip the baked potato that evening but select Wednesday night's spaghetti. I race against the mounting anxiety. I reach Sunday. It reaches its peak.

Suddenly, it dissipates as I almost laugh out loud at my last dessert. My options are:

Apple crumble

OR

Animal crackers and chocolate pudding

I can take a hint. I make my selection and submit my menus immediately. Quick, before my brain catches on and I chicken out.

The nutritionist leaves with the forms and I realize what I have done. This week, I will be eating food. Not just any food: mac and cheese. And fries, a burger, spaghetti, chocolate pudding. This may be catastrophic.

Too late now; the forms are gone with the nutritionist. The girls move back to community space. I want to thank Emm for her help, but her spot is empty.

35

They had arrived early. Matthias checked in. They watched his suitcase roll away on the carpet; he would pick it up in the States.

He turned to Anna:

Breakfast?

Yes, breakfast. Always breakfast, her favorite meal of the day. Their last meal together until she followed him to America in a few weeks.

There had to be a Paul, somewhere. There was always a Paul somewhere. They found a Paul, she found a table while he pulled out his last coins. He did not have to ask her what she wanted: a pain au chocolat, *and one for him.* Deux cafés: allongé *for her,* crème with two sugars for him.

They had their last breakfast Chez Paul together in Charles de Gaulle Airport, Terminal 2E. Cream on his lip and his hand on her knee. She kissed both and finished the crumbs.

36

I remember that breakfast,
Matthias says, his hand on my knee.

Thursday evening, visiting hours. This time we are in my room.

I remember that breakfast too, just not how it tasted. I watch myself eating, licking, loving the *pain au chocolat* like watching myself on film.

Anorexia is not present in that memory; I could still eat and enjoy food. I could still recognize the texture of light, flaky pastry on my tongue. I could still savor good chocolate spread. Now that memory tastes bittersweet. Actually, it does not taste like anything. I have no taste buds anymore.

After years of restriction, my brain, with effort, can identify three flavors: salt, sweet, and cotton. All three disagreeable, but cotton is the one I fear least. So I choose it every time, by default, to give my anxious mind some respite. Broth-based soups, green salads, popcorn, and apples. No pleasure but no pain at least.

I am told that some taste may be recovered after years of healthy, varied eating. The caveat being that that would require years of healthy, varied eating.

Well, I have my first week of that set. I tell Matthias about meal planning. He looks at me, incredulous:

You've got to be joking.

I feel the same way.

But tonight I also feel, perhaps prematurely, confident. I announce to Matthias:

When all this is over we'll have breakfast, Chez Paul. Pains au chocolat *and coffee.*

But he does not take part in my reverie. He looks out at the magnolia tree.

Matthias, is something wrong?

Still looking out, he says:

No, Anna, nothing's wrong. I am happy you listened to Emm.

But . . .

His hand leaves my knee and he speaks again, suddenly angry:

But I bought black bean burger patties for you, remember? Months ago! They're in the freezer, right next to the frozen meals that do not contain dairy or meat.

I used to beg you to eat them! I even used to set them on the counter before work. All you had to do was put one in the microwave and press the button, Anna.

I did—

Don't lie to me! I know you did not. I take the trash out every night, remember? You used to throw them away.

He had never confronted me. I cannot think of what to say.

And every time we went out I would order a basket of fries just in case, just in case you would eat one. One fry, Anna! Or one of my pizza crusts!

His voice is turning hoarse.

Our fridge is full of yogurt! We have cereal and oatmeal and toast! I used to beg you to eat! I used to fight you to eat!

We stopped fighting!

Yes! Because I gave up.

His hands to his face. After a while he runs them back into his brown hair. I used to do that. His breath escapes, jagged. He calms down and finally looks up.

His voice is quiet now:

I'm sorry, it doesn't matter. I'm glad you listened to Emm. This is a big step for you, but I think you can do it. You will have good support next week. It's just . . .

He looks out the window again. I want him to finish his thought. I reach for his hand:

Hey, you can say it.

He looks back without seeing me.

Just . . . why was I not enough?

I do not know.

Why Emm and not me, Anna? Why did we have to end up here? Why did it have to get to this for you to start to eat?

I do not know why I never touched his fries or why I threw out the food. I do not know why I lied every time he asked me about lunch. I do not know why I tried to starve myself and why I am eating now.

I have no choice here but to eat; they took my freedom away. You loved me too much to do that—

I nearly killed you,

Matthias interrupts.

His jawline is taut and a vessel is pulsing madly at the base of his neck. His hands are in fists. I hesitate before touching them lightly:

Hey . . .

Sobs. His and mine. In Patient Bedroom 5 of a horrible place called 17 Swann Street.

You brought me here. You saved my life,

I tell Matthias, still crying. I am sorry,

I am so sorry. I do not know why or how it got to this.

I don't know why either,

he whispers,

but I'm here.

I am here too,

I promise. And to keep fighting this.

We hear Direct Care's heavy footsteps and panting come up the stairs. Visiting hours are almost over. Matthias stands up.

Noses blown, eyes dry now, he asks:

When all this is over, Chez Paul?

I swallow my saliva and fear:
Pains au chocolat *and coffee.*

He leaves me at 17 Swann Street with my evening snack and myself. And a week's worth of food to swallow that I have not tasted in years. I do not have to remember or like them, I just have to try. I just have to chew and swallow, chew and swallow, one cotton bite at a time.

37

Sunday. I have been here a week, and to my surprise, am not dead. I lie in bed, relishing the first few minutes and rays of the morning.

I reflect on my first week at 17 Swann Street. The psychiatrist had said that I was depressed and my brain was hungry and irrational. *Hungry Brain Syndrome:* the reason I was constantly cold, sad, tired, paranoid, angry.

The nutritionist had said that I was undernourished and that I had to eat. Dairy, and oil and grains and beans and tofu and nuts and granola and eggs. She had even suggested junk food. She was mad.

The therapist had said I repressed my feelings. I had explained I have none. Unless she counted feeling cold, and tired, and empty, and sad. I had explained I have no energy for superfluous things like feelings. What little food I ate I used to survive; no leftovers for hormones or tear glands.

Are you happy?
she had asked.
I had shrugged.
Angry?

Shrug.
Are you sad?
Shrug.
What do you feel like doing?
When?
Today, tomorrow, with your life?
Her questions had felt tiresome and irrelevant.
Do you feel hopeless?
I had cried.

My diagnosis was anorexia nervosa. My insurance had agreed and had authorized my stay here till I was restored to a healthy weight. The primary care physician had examined my test results, and was concerned with my heart, brain, stomach, kidney, pancreas, liver, bones. Just those. But she had not addressed my dormant ovaries, so I had brought them up.

I had told her I could not remember the last time I had a period. A few months, perhaps years ago. But I did want a baby, so could she please tell me:

When will my periods return?
She had not replied.

I had completed three meals and three snacks every day of this week. None had been popcorn or fruit. I roll onto my stomach in my one-person bed and breathe into the pillow. Hello Sunday.

I am not particularly religious, but I had asked for a church pass. My treatment team had promptly endorsed this spiritual supplement to my nourishment. All I had to do, I was informed, was get through breakfast and a snack, and Direct Care would drive me to mass at 10:30 A.M. I could do that.

So, after the midmorning snack, Direct Care hands me my phone. Then she, I, and one of the other girls step out into the parking lot.

The girl's name is Sarah. She had come in on Friday. Exceptionally; patients usually come in on Mondays but, as Emm had explained,

The weekender's bed was free.

On the day she had arrived at 17 Swann Street, her hair was the first thing I had noticed. Fiery, and it matched her lipstick, I had noted with envy. I own three tubes of red lipstick myself, but I am too vanilla to wear them. I watch Sarah wear hers, her hair, and her Southern drawl with showstopping confidence.

Today she is also wearing a long flower-print dress and a pair of Marilyn sunglasses. She sways toward the service van sensually. My blue jeans and hair in a bun follow. We climb in the back. Door shut.

Direct Care starts the engine and we drive off to church. I do not anticipate the rush of emotion that follows.

It fills my lungs suddenly as the van backs out then turns right on the street. From my bedroom window on the east side of the house where

I have been for a week, I could only see as far as the curb. Now it is behind us. Now I watch the houses and gardens roll by, not realizing just how trapped I had felt until a tightness in my throat disappears.

The drive is short. The church is an unremarkable building five minutes away. There is a wide parking lot on its right, a green field on its left, so green against the spotless blue sky, I want to lie in it. We are dropped off and told we will be picked up in an hour, at this precise spot. Then the service van leaves us, stunned and free, and slightly disconcerted on the sidewalk.

For a moment Sarah and I just look at each other. We do not know what to do with ourselves. We have an hour to blend in as normal church-goers, but how does one do that? Surely someone is going to recognize us: runaways from *that* house. The one where they keep the girls who cannot eat. We walk to the entrance hesitantly.

So far so good, until . . . we are stopped, by a well-meaning matron and a heaping tray of hot coffee and doughnuts. Sarah and I freeze, but only for a second. We then politely refuse and walk on, smiling at each other furtively. Blending in, blending in.

The big hall is lined with stained-glass windows, colored light pouring in. The ceiling high enough that from it could easily hang a trapeze. We slip quietly into the last pew just as the choir begins to sing. It is glorious. Music. It drowns out everything: the psychiatrist, the nutritionist, the therapist, Direct Care, my family, Matthias, the sadness, the anxiety, the fear. Every muscle in my body feels like it is unclenching. I can breathe. I do. I could be in a mosque, a synagogue, a temple. I could be on a mountaintop.

I do not know if anyone hears prayers. I decide to pray anyway. I let my shoulders slouch, my back bend, my ankles uncross, and myself be completely honest.

I am not depressed. I am sad, because I am away from those I love and every day without them is a day lost. Because I lost a brother and a mother and know what a day lost means.

I am not undernourished. I am starved for a meal I would not have to eat alone. For someone to love me and tell me that I am more than enough, as I am.

I am not anorexic. I am out of control. I know it but I cannot stop. I am a child in a body that grew up too soon, found adulthood and real life a scam, and now is trying to lose enough weight to lift off the ground, fly away.

As for my body, I think it is fine. It and the world just disagree. If only my ovaries . . .

I notice a little human crawling on the floor by the pew. Little fingers, little feet in their little blue shoes. He looks up at me.

His mother clearly dressed him in his Sunday best this morning: a pale blue and white checkered shirt with a little clip-on tie. His pants are kept from slipping off by brown suspenders on which graze little giraffes. He seems content enough to waddle around, floor-level, examining shoes and handbags curiously, searching for things to put in his mouth.

I crouch down to his level. He interprets my move as an invitation to play. He reaches out to me with the open hands and smile only toddlers in this world seem to have. How can I refuse such hands? I sit down, cross my legs, and we play peekaboo while the faithful congregation prays on.

38

Let's make a baby,
  Matthias said.
Sure,
she said.
Let's.
It was raining in Paris in June. They were looking out the window, sipping their coffee. Anna laughed at the surprise on his face.
Really?
Really.
It was an easy yes. Of course she would make a baby with him.

After Camil she had decided she would not have children of her own. She had seen what his death had done to Maman. So no. No children, bedtime stories, lullabies, treasure hunts. No nightmare banishing, birthday cakes, no Sunday morning cartoons. It was too messy, it hurt too much.

  Until she had met Matthias.
Let's make a baby.
Yes.

How many babies would you like?

Two. Two boys. Or two girls. Or one of each. I don't care.

Whatever the sex, we will teach them to ski. Oh! And play tennis! And the piano!

Ballet classes for the girls, like their mother, *Matthias added.*

Of course, and tiny trainers that match yours.

They will speak many languages and be very intelligent.

And be good at math!

She was counting on their father's genes for that.

Let's make a baby then,
she told Matthias.

We'll start in Saint Louis,
he smiled.

Neither Anna nor Matthias had heard of amenorrhea then. They soon did: the absence of menstruation for at least three months.

Or more.

They both pretended not to see the reason right in front of their noses, on her plate; a body that can barely sustain itself is not qualified to hold another.

Severe calorie restriction and low weight cause hormone levels to drop. No more cortisol, leptin, LH, FSH. Without those, no estrogen. Without estrogen, no egg, and with that no need for a uterine lining. What for?

No period for more than three months. Or twelve. Or twenty-four.

They kept trying anyway, but the more weight she lost, the less Matthias mentioned a baby. In fact, the less keen he seemed on wanting one, or her in general.

She was angry. She could have blamed her disappearing curves, breasts, lips, thighs. The insufficient food, the absence of fats and protein in popcorn and apples. She could have blamed all the running or, more simply, anorexia. But that would have meant acknowledging anorexia. Instead, she blamed Matthias.

Deep down, honestly, she blamed herself. For not being enough. Beautiful, sensual, or just good enough to be a mother. But she fought the sickening thought with denial and the anecdotal evidence that some women with anorexia could and did conceive,

and clung to that fantasy so desperately that she took a pregnancy test every month.

39

We step outside to find the van already waiting for us. Sarah and I enter and do not speak. Neither does Direct Care, thankfully. I had once been more outgoing. I used to laugh, ask questions, flirt. These days I find myself shy around people, out of body and place.

I glance at Sarah, next to me in the back seat. She looks like a movie star, and not at all like she suffers from an eating disorder. Or like she suffers from anything. Then again, I have been at 17 Swann Street a week, long enough to know that every one of us has demons, whatever the lipstick we wear.

We park and I stop to soak in some sun before going back into the house. Sarah turns to Direct Care:

Since we got some time before lunch, may we sit outside for a while?

Her vowels trickle like honey, I marvel. I have never heard anyone speak like that. Her hair and lips in the sun are ruby red. I fuss with my own hair.

Direct Care's shrug is taken as a yes. We sit on

a bench along the back wall. I am uncomfortable and self-conscious by this sensual woman, but the sun on my skin is worth it.

I close my eyes.

Sarah speaks:

You like children, then. Want any?

I open my eyes. Sun gone.

I cannot have them just now.

Too blunt. She was just being nice. Damage control:

Do you like children?

I have a two-year-old boy.

I am stunned. A second look at her. I reevaluate her movie lipstick, her age. She looks so young. I try to respond normally:

You must miss him.

Darlin', horribly.

I do not know what to say, so I say nothing. Then she starts speaking, like a stream:

He was a mistake, you know, my Charlie. I named him after Bukowski. I had no interest in motherhood, or in marrying his idiot of a father. I fancied myself an actress. I knew I had talent. But I was born in the wrong place and the wrong body for a star.

The wrong body. I look at her again and wonder what she sees in the mirror.

Where was that?

Oh, girl, in a farmhouse as deep South as you can picture. I had three brothers and two sisters and one very discontented mother who made jam and pies with lots of cream. She had gorgeous red hair that I did not inherit, but I fixed that when I was seventeen.

She gives her hair a coy shake, for emphasis.

Just about the only thing about her I ever envied.

I could easily see her, red hair and lush curves, dominating any stage. But she is not onstage. She is here, at 17 Swann Street.

My boyfriend's name was Sam. Sam. Short and sweet and nondescript, exactly like him. One night, we were chugging stolen beer in his car. I told him I was running away. I wanted to become a star. I became pregnant instead.

So I married him and moved from Ma's house to his.

She laughs bitterly.

I wanted to be anything but her. Instead I turned into her. Thank God I took the jam and pies with me. They kept me company.

Her farmhouse, I note, is my cube on 45 Furstenberg Street. I can relate to her solitude, except that instead of food, I filled that void with air.

But then you had Charlie.

Then I had Charlie.

I did not have a Charlie. I do not have a Charlie. She turns her long-lashed eyes to me:

Why do you want a baby?

Out of body and place again. The best answer is the simplest, I decide.

Because I love Matthias. I want a family with him.

You're lucky.

She is right. I am.

Don't let your Matthias go. Whatever you're here for—anorexia, I'm guessing?—think about what it's costing you.

I do not appreciate her assumption that I chose this disease, or her unsolicited advice. The air cools between us. She must sense it, because she quickly, candidly adds:

I promise I'm not preaching, darlin'. Believe me, I'm in no place to judge. Look at me: I should be spending Sunday with my son. Instead, I'm sitting here.

Why are you sitting here then?

Because in the hours I spent alone with Charlie, I drank, ate pie, whole loaves of bread with butter and jam.

She tells it like a story, dispassionately. Someone else's life.

I tried painting, reading, going on walks, but I always wound up in the kitchen. I rode two damn years on sugar and alcohol, and when I could get my hands on it, Xanax.

She stops awhile in the space of those two years. I do not interrupt. Then she resumes:

Our birthdays are a few days apart, little

Charlie's and mine. On my nineteenth birthday I had whiskey and Benadryl while he slept. When I woke up, Charlie was crying in his crib. Sam was bent over me, pathetically terrified.

I turned twenty last week and he turned two and I had whiskey and Benadryl again. Sam threatened to take him and leave me. Then he up and did it, the fucker.

Sarah is twenty. Sarah is twenty. Just a child in a woman's body. All the makeup in the world will not change that. Still, she pushes her sunglasses up further.

So now I'm here. Not for Sam, but for Charlie. I want to fix myself up before his next birthday. I can't live without my baby.

It echoes between us. *I can't live without my baby.* And I cannot live without Matthias. Matthias who, unlike Sam, did not leave.

Yet. Did not leave yet.

Don't let your Matthias go. The back door opens and Direct Care's head pops out:

Come on, ladies! Time for lunch.

40

Do you really remember?

Every detail. The way you smiled, your ear-rings and that giant scarf you like. My heart was beating like an orchestra.

I feel my cheeks turning pink, embarrassed. I remember that night too.

It was so cold but the lights were so beautiful! Remember? I hid in your coat.

I remember,

Matthias says, his hand in my hair. Then:

When all this is over, we'll go back to Paris and see the lights.

Silence,

but he does not notice, painting his picture in the air between us, on a Sunday night in an upstairs bedroom at an eating-disorder treatment center.

We'll stroll through the Christmas markets, freezing, but I'll keep you in my coat like last time. We'll have mulled wine and buy chestnuts in newspaper cones. And I know you love the displays at Printemps, so we'll go there, and to . . . what was the name of that shop? Repetto? For your ballet shoes? . . . and that pâtisserie by the Place des Vosges, with all the art galleries—

Pouchkine,

I interrupt flatly.

Pouchkine! Yes!

He carries on, along the streets of Paris in his head. But I am still at 17 Swann Street. I cannot leave the Van Gogh room. He eventually stops and looks at me, probably waiting for an answer. I have not been listening.

Anna? Are you listening?

Yes.

Well, what was the name of that song?

I do not know, because I have no idea what he had been saying.

Can we talk about something else?

He is disconcerted, but responds:

Of course. What do you want to talk about?

Anything but the future. Or the past. I had not thought the mention of either would cause such sharp pains in my chest. That Matthias remembers me on that first night, when we met on the Grands Boulevards, when I do not remember or recognize myself, those earrings, that scarf.

When all this is over. The sentence angered me. How does he know it will be? How can he see Christmas lights in May when I cannot see beyond evening snack? I cannot see tomorrow, or myself in the mirror. I cannot see myself at all.

Matthias is still waiting for an answer. I still do not know what to say.

He pulls me closer:

Hey, I'm here. Talk to me. Tell me what's wrong. Did I make you sad?

Not sad, no. Just weary.

Sorry, I am just tired.

Do you want me to leave?

I do not know what I want, or rather, do not know how to want anymore.

Anorexia nervosa makes the brain shrink; it cannibalizes itself. It must; it is starved but it must keep working. Gray matter must be sacrificed. My brain must have eaten up the sections where my hope, ambition, dreams were. Thoughts like *when, soon, tomorrow* are fantasies I can no longer imagine.

We used to make plans. I used to make plans.

No, I do not want you to leave.

I want to want something. I need to want something. A baby, a job, a future, a reason to get out of here.

Matthias, I cannot remember. My brain is so foggy.

I try to conjure an image of Matthias and me in Paris, Matthias and me without anorexia. Matthias and me happy. But I only see the photograph on the whiteboard, and I am not even in it; Matthias is disheveled and sleepy, squinting at me, behind the lens.

I keep my voice steady when I speak again, but my chin gives me away:

What if this is not over by Christmas?

Then we'll go to Paris the Christmas after that.

His voice is as shaky as my chin, but his face is adamant. I realize he is telling himself this just as much as he is telling me.

You will remember and get better, and after that, we'll go to Paris.

What if I do not? What if this is it?

This is not it. It can't be it!

We both want to believe him. He lowers his voice:

You don't understand, Anna. That girl from the Grands Boulevards, she's everything to me. You cannot forget her. I need her to exist.

I need her to exist too. I lean into Matthias, both of us still, in the present and in the Van Gogh room.

He smells of musk, my head in the nook of his neck. A freckle. He speaks very softly now:

I know you're fighting hard and are exhausted. I know you can't see the future. But I need to, Anna, or I'll go insane. I'll picture it for both of us, okay?

Okay, Matthias.

I need something to hold on to, and I think you do too. It doesn't even have to be Christmas. How about just next month? Next week? Tomorrow?

After a while, I nod my head into his neck. He breathes out in relief.

Good.

We can hear Direct Care's heavy footsteps on the stairs. Matthias glances at his watch. He turns me toward him and kisses me forcefully on the lips before she comes.

All right, Anna, we have a plan: Focus on your meals, and we'll have a date tomorrow. How about a game of chess? I'll bring the board.

I nod.

Chess sounds wonderful.

We both already know that tomorrow night, he will win and I will stink. There is comfort in that certainty.

I walk him down the stairs. He does not kiss me in front of the girls, but at the front door he turns to me:

I know you don't want to hear it, but I need to say this for me: when all this is over and you leave this place, I will take you on a real date. We'll go wherever you want: a movie, a concert, an art exhibit, dinner. Then we'll come home and I'll make love to you. Who knows, maybe we'll make a baby. Then we'll go to Paris for Christmas.

I nod.

I'd like that.

I miss you. I miss us.

Me too.

He goes home and I miss going home with him. I miss sleeping with him, wanting to.

My brain must have eaten my libido too, when it shut down my ovaries. *A result of malnutrition,* the doctor had said. But also that *with weight gain, according to some studies, some gray matter might be restored.*

41

Treatment Plan—May 30, 2016

Weight: 89 lbs.
BMI: 15.3

Physiological Observations:
   No noticeable weight gain in spite of patient compliance with meal plan. Treatment team estimates this to be normal consequence of the body's exposure to normal nutrition after prolonged starvation. Patient's metabolism likely in hyperactive mode as organ repair commences. Risk of refeeding syndrome is high.

Psychological/Psychiatric Observations:
   Patient appears compliant with her meal plan but continues to struggle with eating-disorder rituals: avoidance of certain food groups, particularly proteins and fats, cutting food into inappropriately small bites, eating too slowly. She has significant fears around weight gain, as well as negative body image, but is working to modify certain habits.
   Patient appears motivated to make progress

toward recovery. Interactions with her husband on daily visits and with other patients appear healthy. Residential treatment remains necessary.

Treatment Objectives:
Increase normal nutrition to restore weight. Monitor for refeeding syndrome.

Monitor vitals. Monitor labs. Follow hormone levels.

Meal Plan Update:
Target caloric value: 2,400 calories daily

42

How was your weekend, Anna?

I am not sure how to answer that. The therapist knows I spent my weekend here, and how that must have been.

It was fine.

I test the waters. Receive silence. I conclude she expects more.

All I did was eat and sleep, and the bed is cold when I am alone.

Do you dislike being alone?

I dislike this question and this couch, and I do not need this session. And I do not have to answer the therapist, I realize, so I do not.

She tries again:

Has Matthias been visiting every evening?

Yes.

You two seem very close.

We are.

We are Matthias and Anna. Anna and Matthias. He eats the olives I do not like. I always take his pizza crust.

You followed him here from France, correct?

Yes.

He would have done the same for me.

A big change.

He was worth it.

He still is. No one has ever loved me like him. Or made me feel so happy and safe. Mentally, I reaffirm my hatred for one-person beds.

Matthias is the best thing that ever happened to me. I am the luckiest girl in the world.

He is lucky too.

No. He is a man who must drive for forty-five minutes every day to see his wife, who lives in a treatment center for anorexia while he lives in an empty apartment. Who comes home to an empty fridge, an empty bed, eats cereal for dinner, from the box. Who does not have children, nor is likely to, because his wife cannot conceive.

No, he is not lucky, but I do not want to argue with the therapist. Monday morning and my second week are not starting off to a good start.

I look out the window. The magnolia tree is there. *So am I,* I think bitterly, *still.* It is still raining; it has been since this morning. That had meant no morning walk. Perhaps that is why I am so irritable with the sweet therapist today.

I'm sorry about the rain,

Katherine says. I turn to her, surprised.

You must have been looking forward to the walk.

Very much.

I do not have much else,

I say, surprised at my own response.

Nothing to look forward to?

she presses,

but I have closed up again. *Not today, Katherine.*

She gets the message. We both turn back to the rain.

My father and I used to walk our dog every morning,

I surprise myself again.

Have you spoken to him lately?

Not since I came here.

Perhaps you should give him a call.

Perhaps, but I will not give her the satisfaction of a response. Besides, it is too late today; staff already has our phones. Perhaps I will call Papa tomorrow on the morning walk.

I calculate the time difference; it will be mid-afternoon in Paris. Yes, I just might. I breathe out a little easier. And chess with Matthias tonight.

43

At 9:10 A.M. on my second Tuesday here, Direct Care walks into community space:

Who's ready for the morning walk?

I am, phone in hand. Emm is already at the door. Most of the other girls are too; Sarah with her sunglasses on, Julia twirling a basketball.

Not Valerie; she remains on the couch, a blanket draped on her thin legs. She is writing, again. I observe she rarely joins us on the walks.

But I have no time to reflect any further:

Come on, ladies, let's roll!

Thirty minutes of freedom, not one to waste. Emm and Direct Care lead the way.

As soon as we are off the property, I call my father, seven time zones away. I silently wish the phone to ring faster. *Allez Papa, allez.*

He picks up by the third ring:

Allo?

Papa?

Anna!

And a bark in the background. I smile: Leopold.

How are you, Papa?

I thought they took your phone away!

They do, most of the day, but I can have it in the mornings and evenings.

He does not mention the dozens and dozens of his phone calls that I missed, saw later and never returned since I was admitted into treatment. Instead, he asks:

How are you feeling? Are you all right? How is the center? Are the doctors any good? Are there any patients your age?

He stops. Then in a strangled voice:

I am so happy you called.

My heart tightens.

Me too, Papa.

I miss you more than I realized. I am so sorry I did not call. I was stupid and angry and ashamed of being here, and I know all these excuses do not count.

Papa, how are you, really?

So much better now that you called. Tell me everything, Anna. Where are you right now?

I smile. He will like this one:

On a walk. We get one every morning.

Ho ho! Lucky girl. Leopold and I are on a short walk too. I just came home from work.

What color is your sky?

That purple gray you like. And yours?

Bright blue after yesterday's rain.

I walk him past the little houses of the neighborhood with their pastel doors. I point out blooming flowers, changing leaves, progress in the vegetable patch. I greet the dogs and rabbits and mothers pushing strollers we cross on our way. I pretend I am elsewhere, on the sidewalk he is walking on with Leopold.

Then I begin to walk him through my first week at 17 Swann Street, but I have barely started when I see the house reappear.

Je dois raccrocher. *I am sorry, Papa. My thirty minutes are up.*

It's all right, Anna.

Pause. Then,

Anna?

Oui, *Papa?*

Silence on the other end.

Me too, Papa.

He says:

Have a good day. Take care of yourself, d'accord? *And call me tomorrow at same time?*

Of course, Papa.

We hang up.

44

He never woke her, but she would hear him shuffle around the next room clumsily, inevitably stubbing his toe against the bed at the same angle every day. He would curse under his breath, trying not to wake her mother, search for his walking shoes and tie his laces in the dark. Then he would peek into her room. Anna would already be up.

As would Leopold, waiting for them both anxiously by the door. Shoes, and often coats, scarves, and mittens on, they would tiptoe out of the house.

The city and time were theirs when they went on their morning walks. Those often began in a silence they had never had to agree on. Quiet breaths and footsteps, his pace matched to hers. Neither would speak before they had turned the corner onto Vaugirard. He did most of the talking then, usually, leading the conversation and walk. Most of the time he spoke of mundane, weekday things and told her random stories.

Today, at the market, make sure you get two artichokes and a few lemons. Do not buy the strawberries. I know you will want to, but wait a week longer. They will taste much better then.

Did you reach the part where Phileas Fogg reaches Bombay? Non? You have been reading too slowly. I traveled to Bombay—they call it Mumbai now—and Calcutta, once. . . .

On their walks, he taught her to smell the rain in the air, to walk slower, to look up. She learned to recognize the different types of clouds, the trees, elegant façades that lined the streets of this city she loved, and all the shortcuts.

At six fifteen they would circle back and stop by the boulangerie, now open, that he liked. The baguette for breakfast, merci. *Quick quick, they would hurry. The others at home would be up and waiting for them hungrily.*

He would stop nonetheless to greet the gardienne *as she swept the entrance of the building, pull yesterday's crumbs out of his pocket to leave in the feed for her birds. Then they would take the stairs, a race of dog, girl, and man. The first to reach the top won the prize: the crusty end of the baguette.*

Somehow, Anna and Leopold always won.

45

My heart feels heavy as I hang up. The walk is over, Papa is gone. The girls linger in the living room while midmorning snack is being set. Some sleep, some read, some color, some knit, some have already begun to wilt. Direct Care collects all the phones for the day and now I am really alone.

I hear a soft scratch outside on the porch. I look at the clock: ten to ten. I jump to my feet. How could I have forgotten?

Girls! The mailman is here!

Emm has already opened the door and taken the letters from his hands. She brings them in and starts distributing them to fidgety, impatient girls. She gives me one too, to my surprise. Who could be writing me? The plain envelope has no stamp or sender's address but right in the middle, my name!

I am ridiculously giddy. Someone has written me! I unseal the envelope carefully.

Dear A.,

I am not good at talking to people face-to-face. I communicate much better with a pen. I don't know why. I guess I just feel distant from everyone else in real life.

I have been meaning to write you again since the day you arrived. I can't believe it's been a week already. I wanted to give you time to settle in, then I chickened out.

I'd still like to be friends, if you would. If not, that's okay.

Anyway, today is Tuesday . . .

The letter is a short and neat page long. Valerie's handwriting is beautiful. She asks about the morning walk. How I am settling in. If I like to read and what. If I want, she can lend me some books.

Just the right degree of personal, just the right degree of formal. Valerie signs her letter "V." I like it. I will sign my response to her "A."

I do not know why she chose to write to me, of all the other girls in this place. Valerie who lives in her books and notebooks and does not go on the walks. Who speaks so rarely and quietly that when she does, it is always an event. Whatever her reasons, yes I do want to be friends. I take a sheet of paper from the communal pile and write:

Dear V.,

Today is still Tuesday, and thank you very much for your letter. I know what you mean about feeling distant from people. I feel the same way.

I cannot believe it has been a week either! You were right about the girls. And thank you for sharing the rules of the house with me.

I am reading Rilke now. I found a book of his in the library. Do you know Rilke? Do you like poetry?

I sign:

Sincerely,

A.

I place my letter in the mailbox on the porch. It seems the most appropriate place. This will be how we conduct our secret letter exchange. After lunch, I sneak a look in the box, wondering if the letter is there.

It is not! In its place, to my joy:

Dear A.,

I do not usually care for poetry, but I think maybe I don't understand it. Perhaps if you explained one or two of Rilke's poems to me?

I haven't been reading much lately. The medication I'm on makes it difficult. I've been having trouble concentrating in general, but I've been writing a lot, so it's not that bad.

V.

Dear V.,

It must be an anorexia thing, this difficulty concentrating. I have the same problem, but poetry helps. Rilke's are short and simple enough that I can get through them easily.

Would you like me to give you one of his poems, before dinner perhaps?

A.

After dinner:

Dear A.,

You were right. It's magical.

Dinner was particularly difficult. The poem helped a lot.

V.

I am glad.

We are in community space again, sitting in post-dinner lull. Waiting for Matthias, I chat with the other girls. Valerie is in her usual spot. She does not take part in the conversation, but she is not isolated. Somehow, she is part of the group. Every girl here has her place.

She looks up from her writing and meets my gaze. I smile. She looks down again.

Doorbell. And chorus:

Anna! Matthias is here!

46

Ninety minutes later, we come down the stairs to much hustle and bustle about the house. It is almost time for the late-evening snack, but on the table, there is nothing set.

Where is everybody? In community space, on couches, cushions, and the floor. Even the nurses and Direct Care. The television is on.

Where have you two been?

Emm squeaks.

You're missing the opening ceremony!

What?

The Olympics!

But that is not until August,

a perplexed Matthias says.

Dude, we know!

Julia exclaims. I almost laugh out loud; by the look on his face, I gather Matthias has never been called a dude.

These are the old ones: the 2012 Olympics! We're watching them again.

What an odd thing to do.

Why?

I ask.

To prepare ourselves for August!

Why else.

It was Emm's idea,

Sarah says,

and Direct Care said we could.

There is something deeply sad about that sentence, spoken by the mother of a two-year-old. But she is leaning forward excitedly, center seat on the big couch beside Emm. Emm, I have not seen this excited about anything since I moved in here; she is staring at the big television screen in the living room intensely, remote control in hand. She turns the volume up over our voices to hear the commentator's remarks. On the other side of her, even Valerie is looking up at the screen from her notebook.

Sit down, you two!

Julia commands, bouncing her basketball from hand to hand.

We'll tell you what you missed.

I'm afraid my time here is up,

says Matthias, glancing at the clock above us.

I'll just leave you ladies to your Olympics and bow out gracefully.

I walk my husband to the door and see-you-tomorrow kiss him.

You'll tell me how it ends?

he jokes.

Of course. Can you handle the suspense?

I return to our bizarre little movie night and sit cross-legged on the floor. The girls are on the edges of their seats, talking, pointing at the screen. The living room, uncharacteristically, is actually bubbling with excitement. I can feel it creeping up on me too; I have not felt such a buzz in a while.

Here's the plan, ladies,

Direct Care says, her serious Direct Care face on.

I will set the evening snacks on the table, we'll pause the ceremony to eat, be as quick about it as we can, then meet back here. How does that sound?

Hilarious, and fine. We inhale our evening snacks. Yes, even I, even Valerie. No one as fast as Emm, though; she is the first back in community space. Within ten minutes we all are too, watching the parade on the screen, gushing and gossiping like a bunch of adolescents. It feels nice. But odd.

Why are we acting like a bunch of adolescents at a sleepover on a Friday night? Why are we watching a rerun of a four-year-old ceremony? I look at the women around me; sick women in a treatment center. And myself. Surely none of them, or I, would be doing this in real life.

Then I get it: real life. For the moment, this is it. Our lives are nutrition, therapy, sleep. Our freedom is confined to our choice of the kind of cereal we eat. The perimeter of our world lines that of the house in which we are living.

In this place the weekly schedule is on the communal board, unchanging. Its highlights include cottage cheese on Tuesdays and the occasional outing on Saturday, apple cinnamon tea, the morning walk, and yoga on Mondays and Fridays.

I look at Emm and see the past four years. *My other passion is the Olympics.* No wonder she is excited. No wonder we all are, by a rerun of a parade.

Gymnasts and runners and triathletes wave flags and circle the stadium. They blow kisses at the camera, at us, on the other side of the screen.

I remember every bit of this parade!

exclaims Emm, all fidgety.

Pay attention, everyone! The Americans are up next.

And the Americans parade next.

That's Michael Phelps! Anna, see him? Michael Phelps!

He is gorgeous. I say so.

I met him that year,

Emm throws in casually,

at the trials. He was nice.

The whole room turns sharply toward her. Punctuation marks pop through the air. Questions are catapulted.

You met Michael Phelps?

You tried out for the Olympics? Did you get in? What sport?

What did you say to him? Was he as dreamy as he looks?

And cruise director Emm blushes profoundly red.

It was so embarrassing: I stuttered, but he was really friendly. I have a picture of us together if you want to see.

Of course we want, we beg to see it! And for more details.

I was trying out as a gymnast,

she explains.

Actually, it was my third time.

She pauses as she and everyone sigh in unison at a close-up of Phelps. Then we turn back to her.

So what happened? Did you make the cut?

Emm's face changes. Silly, hasty question.

No. I came here instead.

We watch the parade end in silence, then Direct Care turns it off. The girls trickle off to their rooms. We had forgotten, for a while, that we lived here.

I remain, as does Emm, her mind still in 2012. She seems smaller in her seat, or perhaps the walls of the living room seem narrower in indirect light. I understand why she had wanted us to watch the parade with her. I understand why she watches *Friends* again and again in between Olympic years.

I understand her anorexia more than she knows,

wings banging on the inside of a cage. But I say nothing; she does not want my understanding. She wants quiet and to grieve.

I should leave her alone. I try, but I made a terrible mistake: I sat on the floor, and now my old lady's bones are locked painfully in this position. She notices me try to pull myself up. The cracking sound of my bones says, *Fail.*

She jumps off the couch and reaches down for my arm. We both pull me up, wincing.

Osteoporosis?

Almost, osteopenia. And you?

Me too.

Of course.

She and I half laugh, half cry. Then we fall quiet, both of us wanting to speak, neither of us knowing how.

I am sorry about the trials and anorexia,

I say.

I used to dance. I hurt myself too. It was not too serious, but I guess I was gone too long. They could not wait; they replaced me.

She nods, then looks at the now black television screen:

I thought I would be competing this year. I spent four years convincing myself I would. That I would be in the parade this August, or at least try out again. Instead I'm still here. Four years, Anna. I'll watch the games on this screen.

The games are not till August, though. You could still be discharged before then.

My sentence is voiced, unintentionally, as a question, to which she answers with a wry smile. The Emm smile. The sad one that broke my heart on my first night here.

I could, but who would prepare the jumbles and lead the morning walk then?

A sad and old lady has replaced the girl whose eyes were sparkling at the screen, just minutes before, proudly boasting about her encounter with the athlete of her dreams. The jumble and the morning walks; she is not joking. *Friends,* the Olympics, and animal crackers. And cottage cheese on Tuesdays.

Emm needs those, and to be the leader of our group, to survive. De facto director of this house. There is nothing for her outside it.

You cannot give up, Emm.

I haven't,

she replies,

I haven't killed myself yet. The jumbles and walks help.

Said in a soft voice. Then,

I'm tired. Good night, Anna.

She expects no empathy from me. Or comfort. She has the Olympics.

And the jumbles, and the walks, and Gerald the Saint Bernard. I head toward the stairs.

Good night, Emm.

215

47

Mother and daughters on a ladies' night out: Anna and Sophie's first ballet. It was still quite chilly for a June evening. Maman was wearing her salmon coat. Over their new dresses, the girls had matching white princess coats that covered their joyous fidgeting.

Maman's fingers had coaxed the knots out of Anna's thick blond hair and pinned it into her first bun. It was the most magical night of her life: Swan Lake. *Anna had fallen in love.*

The stage, the lights, the audience blackened out of sight. The violins flooding the hall, the music filling her lungs. Pas de bourré, pirouette, glissade, grand jeté. The closest anyone could come to flight.

She left thinking ballerinas existed only in that enchanted, chandelier-lit world of red velvet seats and carved wood painted gold, undulled by grimy city light. That place, and the swans' delicate white feathers, filled the daydreaming six-year-old's head. So Maman took her to ballet lessons once a week, then twice a week, then every day. To rehearsals and auditions, and she and Papa applauded proudly at every curtain call.

Anna became a ballerina like the ones she had dreamed of, and she found out they were real. Up close and offstage, they were competitively, painfully thin as well. They sweated and stretched for eight hours a day, went to bed aching and starved, but when the curtain went up at 8:00 P.M. every night, they turned into swans.

She also found out that she did not have the body of a perfect ballerina. She was just a little too short and her feet were a little too flat. And she could stand to lose a little weight, she was constantly reminded. But she was good and disciplined enough that she could entertain the dream that if she pushed a little harder, stretched a little further, spun a little faster, she could change.

She did her pliés, put more fire in her jumps. Glissade, glissade, grand jeté. Back straight, shoulders back, ankles crossed. Always. The lighter she was, the easier it would be to flutter off the ground. So the less the other girls ate, the less she did too. Dancer see, dancer do.

Anna neither flew nor grew taller; she got shorter as her spine collapsed. Her knees buckled one afternoon in rehearsal. Surgery at twenty-three, then bed rest.

48

Wednesday begins stickily humid and disconcertingly hot. Disconcertingly, because I have anorexia, and anorexics never feel hot. Today I am, uncharacteristically, sweating, though my hands and feet remain cold. They are always cold; poor peripheral circulation. *Acrocyanosis*, the doctor had called it.

Otherwise known as the inability to hold a chilled glass of champagne, or Matthias's hand, because I cannot afford to lose what little heat I have. Or wearing two pairs of socks under layers of blankets in the summer, shaking for hours, unable to sleep. Acral coldness. As lonely as it sounds.

The day does not improve as it progresses; I am served half a bagel and a mound of cream cheese for breakfast. Consequently, the morning walk is miserable. I am short with Papa on the phone.

I change into clean and dry clothes when we return. My irritation is harder to shed. However, just then I hear the door and the mailman. My first smile of the day.

I wonder if V. wrote to me.

She did!

Dear A.,

I think I like having a pen pal. Last night was fun with all the girls. It was actually my first time watching the Olympics, but don't tell Emm!

I saw you struggle with the bagel and cream cheese at breakfast this morning. It's a difficult one for me too. But we did it. They say it gets easier with time. . . .

Across from me, Valerie is in her spot, of course, reading a letter of her own. Her hair is in a tiny bun at the top of her head, like mine. It looks even smaller, and so does she, compared with the sweater she is wearing; two sizes too big at least, I guess, and obviously a man's. Boyfriend? Father? Brother? Too early in our friendship to ask. *Perhaps in a few letters,* I tell myself as I reach for a sheet of paper from the communal stack, when—

A shriek.

We all look up and around. Valerie, holding her hand up: paper cut. The letter she had been reading and its envelope are on the floor. Her index finger is red and bleeding abundantly all over the place.

Asteatotis: dry and scaly skin. Another symptom of anorexia.

The condition can lead to profuse and prolonged bleeding from superficial cuts. I know this from experience; a pair of scissors, a knife, a sweater that is a bit too rough, air that is even slightly dry or cold, the edge of a letter or envelope . . .

And blood is flowing everywhere: on her hands, down her sleeves, on the sweatshirt. Emm is the first to react. She runs to the nurse's station for supplies and help.

Sarah withdraws, feeling faint. Julia is staring curiously. I take Valerie's hand and with a wad of tissue paper try to blot the blood.

Her hands.

Pellagra. Hyperpigmented and scaly plaques. Vitamin or protein deficiency.

Lanugo. Downy fine hair, to preserve body heat, covering the entire body.

I would not notice either, normally; Valerie always wears long sleeves. The nurse and Direct Care arrive and take over. My red tissues and I step aside.

Valerie is swept out of community space before any of the other girls faint. Emm, of course, is right behind Direct Care. The rest of us wait.

Just a cut, dear, but we must clean it.

We can all hear the nurse's voice.

You may need stitches. Let me see. Pull up your sleeve.

Suddenly, her voice is silent. For a full minute, then,

Emm, thank you for your help, now please leave. Go back to community space.

I am surprised not to hear her object to this. Emm returns with a look on her face I have never seen before.

Are you okay?

I ask.

She nods.

Is she?

She hesitates. Then, as if she were dropping something very heavy, she whispers:

She cuts.

Dermatitis artefacta. Skin lesions, ulcers, bruises, scars. Valerie, placid Valerie, cuts herself. How could any of us have guessed?

Her possessions are still on the floor, but my hands are still stained with her blood. Emm picks them up before I ask her and sets them in Valerie's spot.

The letter she was reading sits, face up, staring me in the face. My curiosity wins over my well-bred discretion. I do not touch it, but from where I sit:

Dear Valerie,

Happy birthday, sweetheart. I'll be in town this weekend to celebrate.

I look away. I should not be reading this. She had not mentioned her birthday.

Soon, Valerie, good as new, returns. I am allowed to wash my hands. Back in community space, I hesitate: what had I been doing before this?

My letter to Valerie. My blank sheet of paper. Suddenly I have nothing to say; Valerie's hands put yesterday's Olympics and this morning's breakfast into perspective. Whatever I write now will be insignificant. But I had promised I would. I think of how happy her letter had made me only a short while ago.

I could write this girl a thousand superficial letters, except I know her now. I know it is her birthday and I know she cuts. Pen to paper:

Dear V.,

That paper cut must really sting. I hope it heals quickly.

May I ask whose sweater you are wearing? Does it mean something to you?

You do not have to answer my questions. I know they are personal. I would just like to get to know you a bit better. If you are willing. I like having a pen pal too.

A.

49

She cut herself, again. Stupid apple, stupid fingers always in the way. Anna reached for a paper towel to blot the blood. It seemed to be gushing out a little too profusely for such a tiny cut. Lately those had been taking longer than usual to heal.

She looked, frustrated, at the half-diced apple on her plate. It was covered in blood and now inedible. She would have to start all over again.

She prided herself in how finely she could cut an apple into little pieces. The smaller they were, the more bites she got per apple, the longer an apple lasted.

She reached for another paper towel and wondered if they had any Band-Aids left.

50

No response from Valerie all day and it is now time for dinner. I think I pushed too hard. We form two lines at Direct Care's instructions to walk to the house next door.

I make it a point not to stand next to her. Space. My way of saying that she has the right to be left alone within her boundaries.

She comes to me instead and slips a note in my hand just as we reach the dining room. I lag behind the others and open it; I simply cannot wait till after dinner.

Dear A.,

I'm sorry I didn't write back. I've been in my head all day.

The sweatshirt belongs to my father. He's coming to Saint Louis this weekend.

She does trust me. I stare thankfully at those two brief lines.

Anna! Everyone's waiting for you!

I hurry in and take my seat. Everyone else has already taken theirs.

Finally, Anna! Dinner is getting cold, and it is absolutely delizioso *today!*

"*Delizioso*," of course, is a debatable term, but Rita is in such a good mood that I do not challenge her. I even dare hope she is right.

Of course, that hope promptly dissipates as soon as dinner is revealed: a heaping plate of spaghetti marinara, with basil and mozzarella cheese. On the side, a garden salad concealed under a hill of cheese and doused in olive oil. Of course. I rue my overconfidence at meal planning last Thursday, and do not even try to recall what I had circled for dessert in my folly.

Valerie's plate is set on the other table. I am disappointed. Not that we would have been able to talk even if we had been seated together. Every girl for herself tonight, and the pasta. Even Emm does not pull out the charades. I focus on surviving the salad and its dressing first. Then the spaghetti, the cheese, the sauce. One bite at a time. I keep my mind firmly elsewhere. Done.

And then, spumoni.

One of the girls is crying and Valerie needs her frozen orange. Julia and Sarah fare a little better; non-anorexics: different demons. They try to lighten the mood with a few jokes. The rest of us listen gratefully. We all wait until the last girl makes it to the apple cinnamon tea.

No one dies, and somehow, the hands on the clock hit seven fifteen. We lie to Rita about dinner being wonderful and walk back in the sweltering heat.

On the way back, I find myself next to Emm. *I'm proud of you,* she says.

Just that and just out of the blue. I turn to her: *Thank you. I did not think I could do it.*

You can. Just don't stop.

I want to tell her, *You too.* But we reach the house and I have infringed on enough privacy for one day.

Back in community space, my hand in my pocket feeling Valerie's letter, I wonder whether I should write back or just talk to her. A glance in her direction: she is staring out the window, her big squirrel eyes vague. I walk up to her; I can always write if she turns me away.

Are you okay?

She does not look it, nor does she look at me. Her chin quivers; response enough. But she remains quiet, and I hesitate. Perhaps she just wants to be alone.

I turn around, but she blurts out,

He doesn't know I am in treatment.

I sit down. Exhale. Of course he does not know; anorexics are selfless lovers and masters at painting rosy lies.

He thinks I came here for a job.

She shows me his letter, now with little blood-stains across on the top corner. He signed it:

Always proud of you, Valerie.
I love you.
Dad

I hand the letter back to her, unsure of what to say. Rather, unsure she wants to hear it. I finally do:

He deserves to know, and I think you need him now.

I look at her. Emaciated and so terribly pale. She has not had a visitor or left the house since I came here.

Valerie is quiet. I wish she would talk to me.

Please tell him where you are. He will understand.

Faux pas. I can see I crossed a line.

Not every father does,

she says.

No, not every father does.

Valerie does not look angry at me for my transgression. She just looks tired and sad.

I was always an A student. I am an Ivy League grad. I am my father's perfect, only daughter. Tell me, what do you think he'll say when he finds out about this?

"This" is anorexia, and 17 Swann Street, but she also pulls her sleeve up, just enough for me to see the start of a thick and engorged red scar. The skin along her entire arm is mangled. She covers it and whispers jaggedly:

His perfect girl lies, cuts, and cannot eat. Why on earth would he be proud of me?

I understand. I think of the men I tried so hard to be perfect for. Philippe, pretending not to know me in public as he stood by his beautiful wife. Matthias, taking my hand and introducing me, proudly:

Have you met Anna, the love of my life?

Valerie is not looking at me anymore, away in her mind, out the window.

51

They were married. They were married! What a cold and happy day. They cut through the frozen park and raced the six flights of stairs up to the flat. They spent the evening talking, playing music, making love. Making plans for the coffee they would have the next morning. They would have it in bed. Then they would have breakfast: eggs, sunny-side up for him, scrambled for her, basil, tomato, oregano. She would make those while he went downstairs to get the baguette.

She went to sleep and was happy for an entire night. But the next morning she woke up at five with a nauseating stomachache.

The boy she had married was still sleeping next to her. On her finger, the delicate ring. What if he woke up and realized his mistake? That he deserved better? That she was not what he had signed up for? The ring was glistening rainbows.

His sweatshirt on a chair, her pink trainers by the door. She slipped both on and snuck out. She began walking briskly in some, any direction, across the park, beyond the park.

Matthias's wife could be nothing less than perfect: smart, beautiful, thin. Anna wore trainers, no makeup, big book lover's glasses, and her hair in a messy bun. He loved that about her, now, but would he still in a year? In a year, in his eyes, would she still be "Anna, the love of my life"?

The stomachache worsened. She thought of Philippe. Who had found her pretty, just not enough. Smart and elegant, but not enough. Philippe, who had told her "I love you" and "Do you really want that slice of cake?"

She had cut her lettuce into smaller and smaller bites, let her hair down, lowered her voice, straightened her back. But she had never met his mother or licked ice cream with him, fit in his mold.

Philippe had not loved her. Matthias did, and she him. He made her blissfully happy. He deserved to be happy. He deserved smart, beautiful, thin. She would be smart, beautiful, thin for him. She would be the wife he deserved. Matthias would be proud of her. She was out of breath.

The wind had picked up and the sky was overcast. Anna stopped and looked around. She did not know this neighborhood, had no key, money, or phone. She had not realized that her walk had turned into a run.

52

Thursday, fresh start. To prove it, the sky rains, washing away yesterday's angst and heat. I can hear the droplets tipping and tapping at the window of my Van Gogh room. I have just returned from weights and vitals, discarded my flower-print robe, and now, back in bed and in my pajamas, close my eyes. This reminds me of Paris.

Today will be a good day, I decide. I shower. Peach blush and perfume. I come down the stairs early for the occasion: coffee, breakfast, and the jumbles. And art class this afternoon.

None of the girls must be in the living room yet; no sound except for the rain. I walk in and jump: Valerie! Valerie, standing in the middle of the room.

Valerie, not moving, feet apart, in a daze. At first I do not understand. Then I smell it, see it, feel nauseated: Valerie has soiled her pants.

Valerie, sweet Valerie, who was so kind to me on my first day. Valerie, whose handwriting is elegant and cursive, standing in a brown mess. I am ashamed for her and look away. Whom should I call? Direct Care? What should I say? I wish Emm were here. Or Maman.

I run out for help then return as quickly as I can, scared to leave her alone too long. An unnecessary precaution; she is still in the same spot, gazing blankly at the wall.

She does not seem to notice I am here, or the smell, or Direct Care trying to clean her up. The look on her face turns my insides cold: nothing. Valerie is not there. Direct Care's sympathy itself is half-hearted. She is slightly overwhelmed this morning; she has breakfast to orchestrate, medication to distribute, and an important announcement to make.

Today is CPR training day, ladies,

she tells us half an hour later. We are all seated, Valerie's pants are clean, and breakfast has finally been served.

In between your sessions, you may notice staff practicing resuscitation techniques. This is just procedural, don't worry. We do this once a year.

The girls seem disconcerted, except for Emm, and Valerie. Valerie does not seem to hear or care. She is chewing and swallowing mechanically. She does not look up. No one knows about her little accident except Direct Care and me.

And Direct Care has other things to think about. I, however, am a mess. My breakfast is too; I spill my Cheerios on the floor. *Valerie and the CPR training dolls.* The latter are

236

displayed flagrantly, unsightly, on the living room floor for us to see. I notice that the inflatable mannequins are fatter than most of us.

The safety measure is disturbing. Why is such training even needed? Naively, hopefully, I reason:

No one could die here.

Nonetheless, my earlier confidence in today being a good day wavers. And I can still hear the rain outside. My heart sinks: *No morning walk.*

But, just as breakfast is being cleared, the pitter-patter stops. I look out the window, incredulous. So does Direct Care. The rain has stopped!

Well how about that? You lucky, lucky girls. Looks like you'll get your morning walk after all.

We dash for our walking shoes and to the front door before she and the weather change their minds.

53

We return from the morning walk, stepping on the lawn, just as the sky begins to cloud again. The first few droplets fall. Direct Care and Emm hurriedly lead the way back in. The rest of us follow close behind, Papa and I chatting along, in French, about trivial, mundane, pleasant things across the ocean and the phone.

I am just about to hang up and step onto the porch, when the tiniest splash of red catches my eye underneath the damp grass. I stop, curious, then drop to my knees and lift the thin green blades carefully.

Strawberries! Two little strawberries, smaller than the size of my thumb!

Papa!

I call excitedly into the phone through which he had been walking with me.

Papa! Papa! The first strawberries of the year!

Julia, who had been strolling behind me, nearly trips over my outstretched feet. The other girls have already gone inside.

Emm! Come back out here! Quick!

They all do, and Direct Care. Even Sarah, but not Valerie. She had not come on the walk.

Sarah gushes over the little gems with me, much to my surprise; I would have thought her too glamorous to get excited over something as trivial. Julia makes fun of me but kneels to look at the strawberries anyway. Emm rolls her eyes and goes back in, but I know she is secretly impressed.

Direct Care goes inside as well; she has a mid-morning snack to prepare. As soon as she does Julia plucks a strawberry and eats it, winking at Sarah and me.

The other girls humor me to varying degrees, but my father truly makes my day: thousands of miles away, he cheers and applauds the beginning of summer on the phone.

My name is Anna, and I have just remembered that I love summer and strawberries. Their presence reassures me; that they can grow, even here, at 17 Swann Street.

Midmorning snacks are already set on the table when I walk back in. I hand my phone to Direct Care and take my place next to Valerie.

Yogurt and granola. Again. Vanilla. Again. Valerie's bowl is light pink. She asked for strawberry. She always does, I realize just now. Valerie, the only girl who asks for strawberry yogurt in this house.

She is quiet. She always is, but she is also very pale. My hand touches her shoulder. She jumps. I should not have.

Sorry, Valerie!

I pull back. Then in a lower voice:

Is everything all right?

No, it is not. It is most obviously not. She does not reply or look at me, her eyes on the bowl of pink yogurt.

I feel sick,

she whispers low enough that Direct Care cannot hear.

I believe her. I know that feeling. I watch her hold back her tears. Direct Care must not notice, and Valerie must not refuse this snack.

Desperate, I look around the table. Emm. What would Emm do? What had Emm done for me when I had panicked at my first meal?

Did I ever tell you about the time Matthias and I rented a car and drove across Costa Rica?

I have no idea why I chose that memory, or how I had dared voice it out loud, but everyone looks up from their bowls and at me, including Valerie.

No turning back.

We wanted to see the Arenal Volcano, a three-hour drive from the coast. We knew we had to get to the crater before eleven, because after that the fumes would cloud the peak and there would be nothing to see, so we left around seven o'clock in the morning and drove across a postcard-perfect countryside.

Out of the corner of my eye, I see Valerie's

241

hand move. It lifts from her lap and rests hesitantly on the spoon to her right. I pick up my own spoon and with the other hand, slowly peel the plastic wrap off my bowl.

Village after village, plot after plot of banana trees. Costa Rica is known for its bananas, you know. We stopped for some and two shots of coffee from a small cart by the side of the road.

She reaches for the plastic wrap.

It was a quarter past ten when we began driving up the narrow road to the volcano. The whole mountain looked like it was on fire in the morning sun. I had my sunglasses on and my hand up to shield my eyes. It took me a while to realize there were no more banana trees.

I make it a point to address the group, not Valerie specifically.

Instead, a carpet of red across the entire mountainside! I could not believe it! The volcano was completely covered with strawberries!

She pours the granola in a single shot onto her yogurt and stirs. I take a bite from my own bowl and continue my story:

Someone later told us that volcanic soil was so fertile that the strawberries that grew there were the ripest and most delicious you could find. We drove past dozens of farmers selling giant crates of them from the trunks of their 1960s cars. Matthias wanted to stop and buy some for me, but we had to reach the crater first.

We did and it was incredible, but the best part was the way down. He bought me an entire crate of strawberries! Oh, strawberries are my favorite fruit.

Valerie takes one bite, then another. I keep telling the story. Whenever she pauses, I remember a detail I had forgotten.

They were so brightly red that we parked the car on the side of the road, sat right there on the grass, and gorged ourselves. They were the juiciest strawberries I have ever had in my life.

I notice Emm watching me, her face expressionless. She knows what I am doing, but I cannot tell if she approves. She looks back at her own bowl and sprinkles more cinnamon on her yogurt.

Every bit of the story I tell is real. The volcano, the crater, the strawberries. Our sticky hands, forearms, and chins. Our grass-and-berry-stained clothes. The fact that for a day, in those strawberry fields in Costa Rica, I was not a girl with anorexia. I was a girl blissfully happy and in love and eating strawberries.

I contemplate my finished midmorning snack and that distant memory. I find it difficult to reconcile the two, and the two versions of me. Valerie and her pink yogurt. Matthias and his crate. Is there really a volcano in Costa Rica completely covered with strawberries?

Valerie takes one final bite and puts her spoon down. I am happy. Emm smiles, or I imagine she does. The minute hand hits ten thirty.

Midmorning snack is over. We all head to community space.

Dear V.,
You did it. Please don't stop.
A.

54

The rain does not stop until just after dinner, in that melancholy half hour of dusk. Matthias takes me outside on the wet porch. We watch the sky change colors. The smell of clean, wet earth is everywhere, and the magnolia tree. It is too lovely an evening to mention CPR training or Valerie.

Rita, the cook, waves goodbye as she walks toward the parking lot.

Ciao, Anna! I'll see you and the girls all tomorrow, at lunch.

Matthias and I wave back. A demain, *Rita, ciao*! Then just the two of us again.

Do you remember Costa Rica?

I ask Matthias out of the blue.

Of course I remember Costa Rica. It was only a few months ago.

It could not have been. Was it really?

It feels like a long time ago.

Matthias says nothing, but I reminisce:

The whole trip was magical. I was telling the girls today about the strawberries in Arenal. You bought me an entire crate, remember? They were so delicious and red—

I remember.

Flat response.

I am missing something.

Is something wrong, Matthias?

No, everything's fine.

Please tell me.

He sits up and looks at me:

It was a beautiful trip, Anna, but it was also very difficult. Do you remember why I bought a whole crate?

Because I love strawberries.

No, because they were all you would eat. Do you remember your legs giving out while we were hiking up to the crater?

I had forgotten that part.

Do you remember the crater?

Not very well.

Anna, you had fainted.

His voice is edgy.

Do you remember the pool?

I do not.

You never went there. It was right by our room and the most pristine beach was less than a minute away, but you were too cold to wear a bathing suit, Anna. The sea breeze made you cry.

I had not even walked on the beach.

Do you remember the all-you-can-eat buffet at the resort? You only ate the fruits, for four days, Anna. You did not even look at the other foods. Do you remember the beach bar?

I do not.

Do you remember the gym?

I do.

He looks very sad.

I remember Costa Rica. I remember seeing an old lady walk toward me and realizing it was you. I remember the day you finally wore a dress and the little boy who saw you and cried. I remember stopping at every fruit and vegetable stand I could find. I remember not being able to sleep at night, listening to your heart, praying it wouldn't stop. I remember Costa Rica, Anna. Do you?

55

Matthias is long gone, and the evening snack. I feel terribly nauseated; both it and my conversation with him are not sitting well in my stomach. I carry the feeling and my thoughts to bed. It takes me hours to fall asleep.

I wake up too soon. The nausea is still there, but that is not what woke me; a rainbow of colorful lights is streaming into the Van Gogh room. I look out the window for their source, onto the narrow parking lot, and my heart sinks as I see the whirling lights of an ambulance creeping in.

A stretcher is wheeled out of the house. I recognize the sweatshirt. Valerie.

I cannot tell if her eyes are open, much less if she is conscious. She is deathly still, but then shakes her head softly to a question she is asked. I breathe a sigh of relief.

I want her to look up at the window, see me looking down. I want to wave. I want to shout out:

Valerie! It's all right!

A promise I have no right to make. Instead, I keep quiet, unable to break the heavy silence of 3:00 A.M.

I watch the team of professionals buckle her in, cowardly behind the window. I am so scared. She must be terrified, and feeling so alone. The ritual unfolds and I hope Valerie can guess that I am attending. The ambulance floods the side of the house, the parking lot, the tree with rainbow light.

Valerie tried to kill herself on CPR training day. The thought gnaws at me like heartburn. A few minutes later the ambulance creeps out of the parking lot and turns the curb.

In the hours that follow 3:17 A.M., I get angry at myself. For having been too scared to let Valerie know I was there. For not having told her it was all right to have soiled her pants and to have cried. For not having comforted her better after dinner. But what would I have said?

That she was not weak for not being perfect? That her father loved her anyway? That she needed him more than she needed to protect him? That she deserved cake on her birthday?

I should have let her know I was there at 3:17, watching from the Van Gogh window. I did not and it is now quarter to five. Almost time for vitals and weights.

Valerie's notebook and her father's letter are on her spot on the couch. I pick them up and put them in her cubby for safekeeping till she comes back.

A few hours later, breakfast again. Served with

anxious gossip this time. Someone says Valerie got hold of scissors. Someone else says it was a knife. I do not want to know; it feels wrong to speculate about the logistics of suicide. I do not mention her father, her accident, or that I saw the ambulance overnight.

After breakfast and the walk I write two hurried letters. The first I copy out three times:

Dear V.,

I do not know where to send this letter, or if you even want to hear from me, but you need to know that I was watching when the ambulance came.

You do not have to come back, or reply. I will understand if you do not. I will save your spot on the couch anyway.

A.

Three copies in three envelopes; there are three hospitals in this area. I address each letter to one of them; I do not know where she is.

To the Attention of Ms. Valerie . . .

It hits me like a punch. I also do not know Valerie's last name.

I feel the bile rise up to my throat as I look around the living room. I need a sign that she was here, that she really existed. Nothing but her notebook and letter in her cubby, and that little space on the couch. She had been so frail that the ungrateful seat had not even kept a mark.

The white blanket had gone with her. Had

it been there before she came? Who and where was the girl who had first brought it to 17 Swann Street? How many girls had sat in Valerie's spot, wrapped themselves in it, and then disappeared? Does it matter?

Yes. It matters. Valerie's last name matters. I find it on Direct Care's list. Her full name is Valerie Parker. She has a father and a birthday. We exist because we matter to someone, to anyone. She matters to her father and to me. There once lived a girl at 17 Swann Street whose name was Valerie.

Someone will have to notify her father. That task falls onto Direct Care. Along with cleaning up patients who soil themselves and practicing resuscitation techniques.

I write my next letter to my sister Sophie. I have not spoken to her in months. Almost since Christmas, since Christmas actually. She had given up on phone calls and texts.

I had been ashamed, too ashamed to pick up; her older sister was a failure. Who could not eat, who would not, even when she begged her. Who made promises she did not keep.

I thought I was protecting her. Now all I can think of is Valerie's dad. His face, the phone call he is going to receive today from Direct Care.

I stare at the page. I have so much to say. I do not know where to begin. I want to start with

I am so sorry and *I love you* and *I miss you* at the same time. I want to ask her how she is, where she is. I want the past few months, years of our lives back. I want hours of conversation with her, but I just have a sheet of paper.

Chère Sophie,

I miss you. I love you. I am sorry I missed all your calls.

Can you try calling me again? I promise to answer this time.

Bisous,

Anna

The mailman takes Valerie's three letters from me and, I hope, to Valerie. My fourth letter will have to wait till Matthias gets me the right stamp.

Emm distributes the day's mail to everyone. No envelope for me from Valerie. The rest of the girls read theirs while Direct Care sets the table for snack.

56

Treatment Plan Update—June 3, 2016

Weight: 91 lbs.
BMI: 15.6

Physiological Observations:
Slow weight gain observed. Treatment team assumes metabolism remains hyperactive. No symptoms of refeeding. Patient appears physically capable of absorbing caloric increase.

Psychological/Psychiatric Observations:
Patient has been exhibiting increasing levels of anxiety and low mood. Disruptions in the center over the past week, including the abrupt departure of a fellow patient, could be contributing factors.

Patient continues to complete her assigned meal plan but has been observed struggling during meals. This is consistent with the recent increase in her target caloric intake. She continues to struggle with strong eating-disorder urges, distorted body image, and low mood. We expect these symptoms to be further aggravated by the progression in treatment course.

Summary:

Patient is still significantly underweight. Residential treatment and further meal plan increases remain necessary. Close monitoring of mood and meal plan compliance is strongly recommended.

Target caloric value: 2,700 calories daily

57

You should not be here on a Friday night,
I say when I open the door.
Not the warm welcome Matthias is used to.
Still, he tries, with a smile:
Well, I was in the neighborhood. I just thought I'd drop by.
But I am not in the mood to smile back. I turn around and head upstairs. Perplexed, but in his usual reserved way, he closes the front door and follows me.
Alone together in the Van Gogh room, he tries to kiss me, but I tense:
I met with the therapist and nutritionist today.
He steps back cautiously.
And?
Well, the first had tried to explore grief in my past, in light of Valerie's attempted suicide:
Do you think of your mother and brother a lot?
I had promptly shut that door in her face.
The second had increased my meal plan and said:
No, you cannot have your dressing on the side,
and that fruit and peanuts do not count as healthier substitutes for peanut butter and jelly.

I had then sat through a particularly painful group session, also on grief. The therapist with the loud smile had been desperate to know how we were processing the incident of the week.

Fine thank you,
had said Emm.

She is lucky not to be here,
had said Sarah.

At least she can ask for seconds at the hospital,
had said Julia, still, always hungry.

I was not hungry. I was miserably full. My stomach hurt after every meal. I was developing an ulcer, I think, because of all this refeeding. I had just had dinner, and dinner had been cheese tortellini. Nightmare. I had once upon a time loved cheese tortellini. And there had been chocolate cake for dessert.

Exposure therapy. Repeated confrontation with a feared situation, object, or memory, used to treat post-traumatic stress disorder, anxiety disorder, or phobias.

Like food.

The purpose of exposure is to achieve habituation. I am not feeling habituated. I have been here for almost two weeks and the meals have only gotten worse.

But I am too tired to tell Matthias that. So I answer:

It went well.

I am lying to Matthias, being horrible to

Matthias, whose only crime is that he loves me. Who could be anywhere, with anyone, tonight, and instead is here with me.

I wish you would not come here every single night. I would rather you do something fun.

Like what?

I do not know! Go to the movies, watch a comedy.

But whose popcorn would I finish if you were not with me?

And the walls come crumbling down.

I cannot stop crying. Matthias just holds me. I no longer have the strength to be cold. I tell him about Valerie, choking on the details, choking on her name.

I tell him everything, sobbing into his shirt. Her father's letter, her arm, her soiled pants, the ambulance last night. When I look up, he is not smiling anymore. He kisses me and this time I kiss back.

We pull away. It is hard to tell if the tears are his or mine. Holding hands still, needing the physical contact, we lie down together on the bed.

He finally speaks:

I am so sorry, Anna. Was Valerie the girl who wrote you that note on your first night?

Yes, and yesterday I had watched her wheeled out of here and away. And today the rest of the world had wheeled on, uninterrupted and undisturbed. Now I am watching Matthias spend another night here because of me.

I am so sorry. I am so sorry,
I cry. I cannot say it enough.
What are you sorry for?
For anorexia. For you here. For interrupting our life.
I am sorry for anorexia, and you here too. But Anna, this is our life.
You did not choose this!
This cannot be the life he signed up for on our wedding day.
Hey, hey.
His arm reaches over me. I missed that weight. I miss that weight.
I chose to be here. I chose this and you and us. I still do. The question is: do you?
Of course I do. I nod forcefully and turn in to the crevice of his torso.
This is so hard.
I know.
It is so hard on you too. One day you will leave me because you can no longer take it, and I will not blame you.
Matthias pulls away and looks straight at me, face dark:
Don't say that. It will not happen.
It hurts too much to know it will. When one day he gets tired of putting his coat around me, asking the waiter to *just steam the*

vegetables, please. Spending Friday nights here.

I am not tired. I am exhausted, we both are, of carrying this disease. One day Matthias will leave because he cannot, should not keep carrying me.

You should not be here every night. Please go somewhere fun tomorrow.

You cannot tell me what to do. Besides, where would I go, what would I do without you on a Saturday night?

Matthias, this is not healthy.

Direct Care appears. Nine o'clock.

Two more minutes,

he tells her.

Please.

Direct Care is human. She looks at both our faces, and to our surprise, says,

You know what? We'll start the evening snack without you. Just come down whenever you're ready, Anna. You won't be bothered.

Door closed.

I cannot believe it, and neither can Matthias. Suddenly, we are both very shy. He speaks first:

You know what is unhealthy, Anna? Not being with you.

We have never played games with one another; our emotions have always been raw. He grazes my collarbone, barely.

I love you. I want you. Do you?

I do.

We make love in the Van Gogh room, and in the small space of that time and that bed, we are Matthias and Anna again and nothing else exists.

Matthias gets dressed and one last time kisses me. A long time since he has like this. He promises to come back tomorrow and opens the bedroom door. I hear him head down the stairs and make my own promises to him silently. Then the ghosts that were hiding just outside, in the corridor, flood the Van Gogh room.

Later, much later, I think of grief and suicide. I understand Valerie. I know why she walked away from the father she loves too much to let down. I lack her courage, though; I cannot push Matthias away. I love him too much, but enough, I hope, that if and when he ever decides to leave me, I will let him go.

And if and when he ever does, I hope it is with someone good. Someone who will make him happy and like roller coasters and ice cream.

58

Saturday morning, and Direct Care announces that whoever wants to go on the outing will have to be at the door and ready to leave promptly after midmorning snack.

This will be the first of the bimonthly excursions I go on. Participation being optional for those, some girls opt not to join. Like Julia, who rolls her eyes:

Manicures? A therapeutic outing? You've got to be kidding me.

Sarah is, naturally, in. As are two of the other girls, and Emm, who answers Julia:

Any excuse to get out of here.

I agree. Today especially; the mood around the house has been tense and apprehensive ever since Valerie left.

I am in no mood for a manicure, but the very triviality of the outing feels like a gulp of air after being held under water. Besides, the sun is out, so at 10:30 precisely, Direct Care and five of us head out.

The road trip only lasts ten minutes in the service van, the same one that drove me to church. It has almost been a week since last

Sunday, I reflect, in the back seat between Sarah and another girl.

Parking lot. Engine off. We disembark and enter the nail salon. An overly friendly lady loudly invites each of us to pick her nail polish. I head to the shelves and shelves of rainbow colors on the wall. They remind me of the lights from the ambulance dancing on my ceiling and walls.

Let's do something fun!

Direct Care suggests to lighten the macabre mood.

We'll pick a color for every girl based on the name that matches her!

That actually does sound like fun.

Miss Emm, you're up first!

After much deliberation, the group assigns Emm: *Turquoise and Caicos.*

For our fearless cruise director!

Plus, it matches the color of her sweatshirt, I observe.

Sarah gets, obviously, *Leading Lady*. And I get *A French Affair*. A girl called Chloe is next. She gets a shade called *Berry Naughty*. Direct Care picks *The Girls Are Out* for herself and *Forever Yummy* for the last girl. She laughs; she suffers from binge-eating disorder, but her sense of humor is fine.

Polish chosen, the manicures commence. Our hands are massaged and lotioned. Our nails are filed, painted, and dried like those of every other lady here.

The salon is full. Typical for a weekend, I think as I look around. Most of the other clients are in their twenties and thirties. Like us. In fact, we almost blend in. Well, perhaps some of us are a bit thin. But otherwise we could be a group of girlfriends getting their nails done on a Saturday morning.

But Direct Care and her glances at her watch are a clear reminder we are not; she is wondering whether we will be back in time for lunch. Suddenly I am jealous of the other women who, after their polish has dried, will have their own lunches in cafés nearby, not portioned, labeled, wrapped in plastic.

This is just an interlude of normalcy, a hiccup in a schedule that hangs on a board in a treatment center's community space. We all know that when our own polish dries, none of us will be going home. The effervescence will simmer down and we will pile into the service van. No keys, no wallets, no phones, no choice, we will be driven back to Swann Street.

The windows are closed in the van and the air is stuffy with breath, polish, and dread. I do not want to go back. To Valerie's empty seat, to lunch, to three courses and a ticking clock, and after the meal, to group therapy.

The van parks in spite of me. We are back, in

spite of us. I ask Direct Care if I may sit outside, just for a while, as I had with Sarah last week. She allows it but warns:

Do not wander off the lawn, and come in when you hear me call. Lunch will be ready soon.

She and the girls go inside the house, leaving me alone.

My exhale comes out a sob, breaths jagged. My hands come to my mouth, trying to muffle any sound I might make. I catch a glimpse of my painted nails. I look the part, don't I, of a manicure-on-a-Saturday lady. One with a life in which she can eat and go anywhere, be anywhere but here.

I sit on the bench, exhausted. The back door opens behind me. I do not bother to turn around. Julia sits beside me.

Bubble gum pops.

So what color did you get?

I show her my nails. They look ridiculous in my eyes now, in the context of this place.

Julia gives me an appreciative whistle that we both know is sarcastic:

Very fancy. Very ladylike.

Both of which I am not, with my hair in a bun and thick layers on. There was no way, I realize, that I had blended in with the other women at the salon earlier.

Julia chews on silently. We stare at the cars in the parking lot.

Wouldn't be caught dead in a place like that. Still, it must've been good to get out.

It was,

I reply,

It just makes coming back here very hard.

Yeah. It's cruel. That's why I don't go. Well, that and I don't do nail things. But seriously, if I ever do leave this place, believe me, Anna, I'm not coming back.

She is serious.

But where would you go?

I ask—more to myself than to her, we both know.

I have no idea.

She shrugs.

Wherever, doesn't matter. Can't be worse than where I am now. Don't even know who I am now.

Me neither. My name is Anna and I am twenty-six and anorexic. I have not always been; I used to want things and do things. Now I am not sure how much of me still exists.

Julia interrupts my thoughts:

Where would you go if you weren't here?

I look at my nails, and before I even realize it, answer:

To the coffee shop by the nail salon.

She laughs. I do too, surprised at my answer.

You wild woman you,

she quips.

And what would you do at that coffee shop, may I ask?

I do not know.

Have a coffee, and read,

I suppose, and watch the people around me.

There would be children on the swings and parents on the benches. Retirees reading newspapers. Dogs and their owners rehydrating, in the shade. And, of course, the ladies with painted nails, gossiping over lemonade.

Julia swallows her gum and reaches into the pockets of her baggy jeans. She pulls out two square pieces of bright pink candy and offers one to me.

Me?

I shake my head politely. No candy for the girl with anorexia, *thank you.*

She raises an eyebrow, pops hers into her mouth. I am a long way from that coffee shop.

She leaves the other piece on the bench between us, in case I change my mind. I look at it; once upon a time I would have eaten it without a thought. I would have enjoyed it, swallowed it, then easily forgotten it. But that was once upon a time ago.

Then I think of the ladies at the nail salon, probably having their lemonade now. They would have taken the candy, said thank you. I take a deep breath. Experiment:

I reach for the piece of candy and unwrap the colored paper,

Thank you, Julia,

and pop it in my mouth before I have time to think.

It tastes heavenly. And sticky and chewy and the sugar is melting on my tongue. I have candy all over my teeth. I chew mindfully, breathe. My anxiety is building up to a heart attack, and there is screaming in my ears,

and it is over. And I am still here, and Julia next to me is smiling.

She nudges me playfully:

Look at you, wild woman!

I do and cannot believe it.

It takes me a moment to catch my breath and finally return her smile.

Are you even allowed to have candy here, Julia?

She winks. We both smile. How wild we are.

Cue Direct Care's voice:

Ladies! Lunch!

Julia jumps up:

Thank God! I'm starving!

I follow her in, but slower, still processing the candy and guilt. And some degree of surprise, I admit: I ate a piece of candy. I did it.

The wrapper is still in my hand. I fold and put it in my pocket. Then I ask Direct Care for permission to wash my hands before eating.

59

Monday was off to a brutal start. 7:15 A.M., every muscle in her body already protesting as she stretched on the floor, warming up in the corner by the resin box. She loved that conifer smell.

And the talcum; both spoke home to her. She had known them since she was six. She had been dancing since she was six. Anna was a dancer. "I am a dancer," she reminded herself.

Except today she did not feel like one. Her stomach was bloated, in knots, and not even the smell of sticky pine or baby powder could loosen it up. She was regretting the bread, the glass of red wine she had had with her salad last night. And the chocolate truffle; Philippe had frowned but she had not been able to resist it.

She had not slept well or enough either, but that is never an excuse. Barre would begin in fifteen minutes, and rehearsal promptly at eight. She wanted a solo part. Philippe had said she had a chance. She believed him.

Just put your mind to it, and lose a little weight.
Just put her mind to it. She had.

Bonjour tout le monde! Everyone gather round please.

The list was in Monsieur's hands. Anna's were cold and clammy. Her stomach-ache had turned to cramps.

Before we begin at the barre, I will bring the suspense to an end. I know that otherwise that is all any of you will be thinking about.

Alors, les solistes: Gaëlle, Daphné, and Gabrielle for the pas de trois. Angela and Michelle, the pas de deux and a solo each. As for the rest of you, I expect nothing less than an impeccable corps de ballet and wish you better luck next year. *Et maintenant, pliés*!

The music began, the piano keys echoing the music she knew by heart. Plié, plié. She was nauseated, but her body had to keep time. It did, because she willed it to. As she had for the past months, practicing, practicing, pushing it further. No complaints. Eat less, stretch more, eyes on the prize: the list.

She would be on it next year. She would just have to practice a little more.

Cambré en avant, cambré en arrière. Relevé, passé, demi-tour. *And again,* plié, plié. *She wanted to cry but did not.*

Passé, demi-tour. Plié.

Her arms were tired. Already? The day had not even started! Eight more hours, and the girls would be cruel in the dressing rooms later.

Philippe would be cruel tonight too. She already knew what he would say. He would mention the truffle and the bread. That is, if she saw him tonight. If he had time; he was so busy lately.

Her stomach hurt.

No more bread and chocolate, she told herself sternly. And no breakfast; she could not stomach it. She would save her banana for later, lunch maybe, and thought of the future, her aching arms, Philippe.

No time for that now, she had to dance.

Allez, on enchaine! Deuxième exercice.

60

Have you heard from Valerie?

I ask from the couch.

The therapist does not answer me. We both know that she cannot.

I do not need details, I want to tell her, *just a sign that she is alive.* And I would like to send her a letter, and the copy of Rilke I finished.

Valerie and I had not had the chance to talk about the poem I had given her. It began with:

Flare up like flame.

And make big shadows I can move in. I knew it by heart:

Let everything happen to you: beauty and terror.

Just keep going. No feeling is final.

Our friendship had been cut short too soon after it had started. An almost friendship. I almost knew her. Julia's words come to my mind:

It sucks, I know, but there are too many of us for me to cry over every one.

Every patient here is a tragedy, but Valerie had been my friend. Almost.

Your concern for Valerie is very thoughtful, Anna,

Katherine begins cautiously. I already disapprove of the word "thoughtful."

but your priority during your stay here should be your own recovery. I'd like you to concentrate on that, can you?

This session and this Monday are not off to an excellent start. The latter is my third here, I reflect. I do not feel closer to recovery. Heavier, yes. *Fatter,* my brain would say. No ground-breaking change at that level.

Two weeks and the novelty of meals and therapy, disconcerting as it was, has worn off. The weekly schedule has become routine. Not the anxiety or sadness, though.

Katherine is waiting for a sign that I have heard and acknowledged her. But I do not appreciate being told what to do, nor do I, consequently, answer.

She tries again:

Why don't you tell me how your weekend went?

No thank you. Instead:

Has anyone told her father yet? He was supposed to visit her.

And I continue Rilke's poem in my head:

Don't let yourself lose me.

Anna,

the therapist warns,

we're here to talk about you.

But I have nothing to say.

That can't be possible.

Rather, nothing to say to her.

I do not want to tell her that I slept with Matthias, for the first time in months, on Friday. That it had hurt but that, for the first time in a long time, I had wanted to. I do not want to tell her about getting my nails done and envying every woman in the salon for the sheer normalcy of her life, having a purpose when I have none.

Are you tired of talking?

Exhausted, I want to say, and sick of being here. And losing what little momentum I had when I first arrived.

I have been talking and eating for two weeks,

I answer.

And if I give up now, I could just disappear like Valerie, in the middle of the night in an ambulance.

What's the point?

I ask her. She responds:

Of getting better? You tell me, Anna.

Isn't there anything you want to do, to be outside of here?

Not really. I cannot dance. I cannot return to Paris. There is nothing there for me. My father and sister have lives that can go on perfectly well without me. Here, my job at the supermarket is almost certainly gone, but good riddance, except for the money, and the hours it filled. So no career prospects.

Matthias does not need me either, not in the immediate, physical sense. He loves me, I know that, and I love him but that alone is not purpose enough.

Isn't there anything you want?

the therapist asks again.

She will not let this go, so I say the first thing that comes to mind:

On Saturday Julia asked me where I would go if I could leave this place.

Visibly relieved that I had said something, anything, Katherine asks:

And what did you say?

I said I would go to a coffee shop, have something to drink, and read.

I reflect after a few seconds:

How sad. I have no goals.

So set some.

I am too tired to answer her. She pushes none-theless:

Can you at least imagine what you would be doing in a world without anorexia?

In a world without anorexia . . . I do not dare dream. But what if I did, in my head?

In a world without anorexia, I would take ballet classes again.

I would find a job I actually enjoy, maybe teach little children to dance.

I would read. Poetry. I would read more poetry. What if I studied poetry?

I would call my father, my sister, the friends I lost in my silence.

I would go home and have sex with Matthias. Over and over again.

Love Matthias. Have a family with Matthias.

But that all remains in my head.

Fortunately, the door knocks just then. Our time is up for today. Direct Care is here with Katherine's next appointment. I vacate the gray couch.

61

Seven forty-six. Matthias is late. Matthias is never late. More irritated than worried, I crane my neck to the right at the window to see farther up Swann Street.

Finally, the blue car appears, signals, and pulls into the driveway. In the seconds that follow, Matthias parks, locks the car, and walks over to the porch, as I debate running to the door before he rings or staying put. I stay put.

Doorbell, and chorus:

Anna! It's Matthias!

I know, and walk over slowly. My petty, hurt way of punishing him; I can be late too.

I open the front door and kiss him mechanically. He looks exhausted. Still he smiles at me.

I do not smile back.

Traffic on the highway?

I ask.

No, actually, long day at work. I'm sorry, Anna. I couldn't leave sooner.

It's fine,

I say. We both know it is not, but the other girls are listening, so we go upstairs to the Van Gogh room and he collapses on the bed.

I close the door and stay where I am.

Your shoes are on my bed, Matthias.

He kicks them off distractedly.

I'm sorry, Anna. Come lie down next to me.

But I do not feel like it.

You could have called,

I say, though what I really mean is: *We only have ninety minutes together! How could you be late?*

I said I was sorry!

he retorts, his voice irritated now.

But Lesley called me into her office for a meeting at the last minute. I couldn't say no.

Lesley. Her name pours over me like a cold shower.

And who is Lesley?

My supervisor, Anna! You know who Lesley is. Why are we still talking about this?

I do not know. He said he was sorry; his meeting just ran a little late. So why do I want to cry? Why am I wasting more of my precious minutes fighting him?

Because I am jealous of Lesley with Matthias. That she gets the whole day with him while I only get ninety minutes in a sterile, confined space. Because I am terrified that one day he will be more than fifteen minutes late.

My throat tightens. My eyes water, but then—

What an idiot I am! He is here, isn't he? He did come! He comes here every night. I rush to the bed and lie down next to him, my arm on his chest.

He exhales, tired, and pulls me closer to him.

I'm sorry. I got jealous of Lesley.

Silly girl. How could you possibly think . . . I don't even know what you thought. I love you, don't you know that?

I hide my face in the nook of his shoulder. I do.

I am just tired.

He sighs:

I'm tired too.

He does not say: *of this.* Neither do I.

62

A Tuesday, again. Still no word from Valerie, and to make matters worse, I can hear Direct Care rummaging in the kitchen:

Girls! Breakfast is served!

On Mondays, Thursdays, and Sundays we have cereal at 17 Swann Street. Those are easy breakfasts. I have Frosties or Cheerios, the first when I win against my anorexia, the second when it wins against me. Fridays are palatable: yogurt and granola. I always have the vanilla. Wednesdays and Saturdays are more challenging; oatmeal and nuts are quite filling. I can get get through them though, plain with almonds, with help from some cinnamon and salt. But Tuesdays, Tuesdays, I dread 8:00 A.M. Not even the coffee helps. On Tuesdays at 17 Swann Street we have bagels and cream cheese for breakfast.

I had declared I disliked bagels and cream cheese on my very first day. I had then stood firmly by that claim in the weeks that had followed. To nutritionist, therapist, Matthias, and Direct Care, I had said I could eat toast instead. With a slather of cottage cheese, if I had to, but not that dense, unhealthy food. I did not like the texture, I did not like the taste. I had said it so vehemently, so loudly, that I almost believed myself.

Almost. In reality, deep in my brain where I knew no one could hear me, I thought it was heavenly. The combination, in one bite, of a creamy, cheesy layer lathered with a butter knife on a warm, toasted bagel, inside still soft, in neat, parallel strokes. A sprinkle of salt, then a sip of bitter coffee with the taste still on my tongue.

It was so decadent it scared me. It could not be right. That first Tuesday, that innocent bagel had nearly made me cry. But it had only been half a bagel, and it had only been my second day. My brain had not caught up with the program, the pleaser in me wanted to please. So I had let the pleaser eat, and when I had finished I remember patting myself on the back and thinking: *It is done.*

But Tuesday came again, and now it is back, and my portions have doubled with my meal plan. Also, as I enter my third week here, my willingness to please is waning. In fact, it is next to gone, worn out by six meals a day. And this morning, mirror or not, the certainty, pulling up my jeans, struggling with the zipper, stomach sucked in, that I am gaining weight.

Breakfast is served. I sit down reluctantly and look miserably at my plate. I see fat and carbohydrates: a full bagel and nearly half a whole pack of cream cheese!

No one can eat this much cream cheese, I think. No one *should* eat this much cream cheese! How will I even fit it all on the bagel? How will I swallow this?

May I have some salt please?

No, Anna.

May I reheat my bagel then?

And have the cream cheese melt onto the plate so you don't have to eat it? Nice try.

I just need something, anything that would make this easier to swallow. But Direct Care has six other sick girls' plates she needs to monitor.

Not a minute over time, Anna.

I cannot eat this. I cannot eat this! My panicky brain screams. I have fought too hard, gone hungry for too long, run too far on sheer will to get here. *I choose what to put, or not, in my body,* it protests, knowing it is not true.

Knowing I have two options at this point: breakfast or the liquid supplement.

A few deep breaths. A nervous look at the clock. I try to calm my racing thoughts.

I must remain composed. Around me, almost insultingly, life is still going on. Julia and Sarah have both finished eating and are on their second cups of coffee. Emm is working diligently on her bagel and the word jumbles. The other girls are quiet; one of them is crying, but all of them are chewing. I must start chewing. I am frozen in place. How do I start chewing?

May I cut my bagel in half, at least?

Sure, Anna.

So I do, and slather some cream on one end and dare myself to take the first bite. Slow, mindful breaths. This is so painful that I almost laugh at the situation. Here I am, about to have a breakdown over a bagel and cream cheese.

I want to recite Maman's poem in my head, but the fear is overwhelming to the point that I cannot remember the first line, or her face. Or ever being this scared. It takes my full concentration just to take a second bite, to swallow it, to take a third. I make it through the first half of the bagel not daring to stop, think, or look up.

Two more bites of the second half remain. About a third of the cream cheese. My heart is about to stop. The screaming in my brain is almost turning me deaf. *No more,* I think. *I cannot.* I did my part. Not another bite. The guilt feels like being dunked into freezing water; I cannot breathe, my stomach is clenched.

Two more minutes to the end of the meal.

Anna, you must finish your plate.

I could force down the last two bites of bagel, but the cream cheese . . . I cannot.

A furtive glance at Direct Care, who is looking the other way. I do not recognize myself doing it: I stuff the cheese inside my napkin.

I wait for the apocalypse. It does not come. No one seems to have noticed. The conversation continues. The clock above my head ticks the last two minutes on. Breakfast is over. We clear our plates. I throw the napkin deep in the bin. Evidence discarded, I ask to use the bathroom. Minutes later, I lock myself in.

I dare to smile at myself in the mirror: Breakfast is done. I survived.

Too soon. Someone knocks gently on the door. I go under freezing water again.

Anna, when you are done in there, I would like to talk to you please.

I take my time brushing my teeth and braiding my hair. I even look out at the magnolia tree. Then I wipe my hands, take one last look outside, noting the sky is bright blue. *Perfect weather today for the walk,* I think. That I will probably not be on.

I open the door. Direct Care is outside, avoiding eye contact with me.

Why don't we talk in your room?

she asks, wanting to spare me a scene.

We go upstairs. Once in my room, she shows me my cream-cheese-filled napkin. I cannot remember being more mortified or ashamed. I admit it is mine.

We have a policy about stolen or discarded food,

she explains uncomfortably. She looks as

distraught as I am. No, not as distraught, not exactly.

I know that policy. I know the house rules; my punishment is a full liquid meal. A nauseatingly thick shake containing the caloric equivalent of breakfast. And another black mark on my record. And of course no morning walk.

The calories. The calories.

I could die right here just thinking of the calories in that liquid supplement. I have never felt anything more overwhelming than this fear flooding my stomach, the room . . . and then the shame.

When did I become a liar and a cheat? What will Matthias think of me? What will he say when he learns that his wife hides cheese in napkins like a thief?

What would my mother say? My father? My siblings, who looked up to me once? What will Papa think when I do not call him as usual on the morning walk?

I can feel something unraveling inside, but Direct Care is still here. I will not cry, or argue with her. I will take responsibility for what I did.

She returns with a large glass of thick, beige cream. Thoughtful, she included a straw. I take the supplement without a word and drink it methodically, all of it.

When the glass is empty I hand it back. She is

decent enough not to preach. She stands up and leaves the room, saying,

You can come down whenever you're ready.

I want to die. Instead, I sit still. Time does too, in the bedroom. I stay there forever, but it is still Tuesday morning when I come down. The girls are waiting by the door for their walk, sunglasses, phones, and trainers on. They all know what happened but do not say anything. I am grateful. They leave.

There is no one in community space, but I need a place to hide. Those are intentionally rare at the house on 17 Swann Street. The bedrooms are off limits by day, the bathrooms permanently locked. There is the laundry room, the coldest room in the house. I go there, curl into a ball, and cry.

I cry more than I ever have. More than when Camil died, and Maman. More than over Philippe. How sad, the power of a piece of cream cheese.

Free fall from a tightrope, and it just keeps going, me lying on the floor behind the dryers. I look up and see the first diet I ever went on and Philippe's beautiful wife. I see that night the wooden stage rose up to meet me and crashed against my knee. I see my brother's empty bed. My mother locking the bathroom door. I see transatlantic flights and two dinner plates set, in a lonely apartment, getting cold.

I see the life I wanted with Matthias, the baby I wanted with him. Every plan and dream that went wrong. Every decision snatched out of my hands.

I see the alarm set for five thirty each morning, after long nights, too cold to sleep. I see fourteen-hour work shifts and thirty-minute runs that got longer and longer gradually. The numbers dropping on the scale. Food groups disappearing with them, along with my friends, ambition, and personality. I see what remained: my apples and popcorn, and my eighty-eight pounds.

I see myself on my first day here, physically as trapped as I felt. I see myself asking for permission to use the bathroom, to step outside on the porch. I see food set in front of me that I did not choose, did not like, did not want. And the yellow feeding tube that will go through my nostrils if I do not comply.

I see every one of those six meals a day and every group and individual session. Then I see the cream cheese and nutritional supplement. But I do not see the point.

My fall ends in a silent crash on that floor. It knocks breath and emotion out of me. The tiny blood vessels in my eyes pop. I am done crying, done trying. I am so tired. I cannot get up.

Not that I have anything to get up for, anywhere or anyone to be. So I stay behind the dryers, on the floor, till the girls return from their walk.

Emm finds me.

There you are. Direct Care is calling us for midmorning snack.

I do not reply or get up, so she pulls me up herself.

Listen to me, Anna: so you slipped. It happens. This is not who you are. That voice in your head that made you do it, that's not you. It's anorexia. It just sounds like you.

Her hand gripping my arm firmly, she leads me to the big wooden table, where the snacks are already set and most of the girls are sitting.

You just need to start recognizing the difference between your thoughts and your disease. You can do it. Try again,

she says.

Try again. I glare at Emm, who does not see me as she goes to her seat across from me. I do not need advice or encouragement from her or anyone else. I do not need a nutritionist, therapist, psychiatrist, Direct Care. And I especially do not need empathy in the form of condescending head tilts.

I have never been more furious in my life. Something in me quietly explodes.

63

Weight: 92 lbs.

BMI: 15.8

Patient attempted to conceal a portion of her breakfast in a napkin and was apprehended. The caloric equivalent of her meal was administered in the form of liquid supplement. Patient was then denied permission to go on the morning walk.

Patient was repeatedly offered sessions with her team therapist, nutritionist, and psychiatrist, all of which she refused.

At 10:00 A.M., patient refused midmorning snack and nutritional supplement shake. At 12:30 P.M., patient refused lunch and nutritional supplement shake. Patient was repeatedly made aware of the implications of each refusal. At 3:00 P.M. patient was given her afternoon snack via nasogastric feeding tube as stipulated by the rules in the patient manual.

Patient has been missing since 4:00 P.M. on June 7, 2016. Search party has been dispatched.

Spouse has been notified.

64

They had known each other less than two months. They were hiding under the covers for warmth, her ice-cold feet between his, on a particularly dreary and dark Thursday in February.

Let us run away,
she said.

Where would you like to go?

Somewhere warm and sunny. I know we cannot afford it.

Who says we can't, *Princesse*? How about Nice?

Somehow, he did find two plane tickets and a little family-run inn right by the sea. No one went to Nice out of season, so they even had a room with a view! It snowed that weekend in Paris, but on the Promenade des Anglais, Anna wore a bright green dress. Matthias, a blue shirt. They made it to the end of the promenade before the first drops of rain.

They were soaked in minutes.

Matthias, there! That little bar!

French fries and socca, *and the house wine*

warmed them up. It was red and sweet and by the time they finished it, they were both very tipsy and the rain had lifted. They walked and danced back to the inn. They kissed their way past it and into a lamppost. They laughed and, still kissing, turned back.

65

I do not know when or how I walked off the porch, across the lawn, and away. Past the other houses, whose owners were ending their day quietly outside. I did not stop to wonder or care what they thought of me and my yellow tube, sticking out of my nose and taped across my cheek, the loose feeding end dangling behind my ear.

I do not know what time it is now, but the sky is losing its light. The air is hot and heavy with magnolia. The tape on my cheek feels itchy. I do not have my watch on me. Or a wallet, or my phone. I left everything at 17 Swann Street, but it does not matter. I am going home.

I am going home to Matthias and my life with him, before this. I will promise him that I will eat and get better, and I will mean it. I will eat.

You will not have to worry about me.

I will throw away my running shoes.

You will see, I will eat.

Yogurt and bread and chocolate desserts and ice cream and French fries and salad dressing.

I will be fine.

We will be fine and we will sleep in the same bed tonight. And in the morning . . .

I run out of breath and lie. My heart pounds faster through my chest. As if to outpace it and reality catching up, I walk faster and farther away from the house. Which way is Furstenberg Street? How long must I walk to get there? What will Matthias say?

What will Matthias do? What will we both do when we come to terms with what I did? What will we do in the morning when we wake up and Matthias has to go to work?

If he sends me back I will hate him for doing it. If he does not he will hate himself. And I will kill myself, slowly and surely, one skipped meal at a time.

My breath is coming out in staccato. I break into a run anyway. I hope my lungs hold strong, not that I am giving them any other choice.

I hate the house on 17 Swann Street. The driveway where Matthias parks. I hate the porch and his back as he leaves it. I hate the thought of him driving away. I hate our empty apartment at 45 Furstenberg Street. I hate my plastic dinners, his frozen ones, my Van Gogh room, our empty bed. I want to run away with him,

but we have nowhere to go.

I sit down on the sidewalk for a minute. For a minute I let myself dream. I dream Matthias and

I run away to Paris, back to our little cupboard room. It is morning in my head; coffee and bread. He plays guitar on the floor. I watch him and distract him with kisses. We get dressed and go for a walk. To the market, where we buy flowers and blackberries. Back in our room, we discard them. We spend the whole day making love.

Then my minute ends.

66

Direct Care finds me. Of course she does. I had not bothered to hide. She returns one missing, gaunt-faced girl with a feeding tube to number 17.

Matthias's car is parked in the driveway. He is standing on the porch. His face says he has been told what happened. His eyes say he does not understand.

I cannot face him. My throat is too tight. My stomach hurts. Bile and shame. I watch him take in the feeding tube plastered across my face. I do not step forward to kiss him; it would have gotten in the way.

Direct Care looks at both of us. Her expression is sad, not angry. She says she is going inside and that we can talk in Bedroom 5.

But I cannot be inside; there is no air inside. I ask if we can stay here. She hesitates, then agrees, saying,

Please do not step off the porch.

Silence until she closes the door. Matthias gestures to the wicker chairs. I sit down on the floor instead. He sits next to me and waits.

I have nothing to say. So he tries:

What happened?

Nothing happened. I let go.

You already know what happened.

Anna, please talk to me. Help me understand. Why?

Why did I hide food? Why did I stop eating? Why did I run away? I laugh bitterly at the ridiculous answer to those questions:

Because of the bagel and cream cheese.

Matthias looks at me like I am mad. He is probably right. I watch him, painfully, fumble with his words and with my distorted thoughts:

Do you mean . . . did they serve you too much? Was the meal too big?

Not any bigger than the day before. Nor any more calorific than the yogurt and granola, the oatmeal and nuts, the Frosties or Cheerios.

Matthias tries to translate my silence into something he can fix.

Was it the taste? I know you hate bagels and cream cheese—

I do not.

He is lost:

But you said—

I lied. I do not hate bagels and cream cheese. I love bagels and cream cheese. The texture and taste are so divine I could eat just that for days.

My voice is rising in tandem with my despair at Matthias's growing confusion. How can he not feel it? How can he not understand? How can I explain my twisted brain?

Matthias, I could eat for days! I could eat for days and not stop! I was fine before I came here because I had forgotten the taste of bagels and cream cheese. And God! I worked so hard to forget, for years! I was so disciplined! I got so good! But today I remembered. All I worked for is gone!

I can hear myself. A foreign, hysterical, high-pitched voice.

I like cream cheese and bagels!

Shaking.

Matthias, what if I start eating them again and never stop?

In contrast, his voice is low, a stranger's. He tries:

Anna, that's not possible. Let's look at this rationally—

I burst into tears.

I burst into tears as I finally realize that this is where this story ends: *Anna, that's not possible.* I wish he were right, I want him to be right, but I cannot see it or believe him.

He tries to reason with me, shout, cry, fight the anorexia in my head. He cannot see or believe, either, that I will never be rid of it.

An hour goes by, of arguing and crying. We are both silent now, exhausted. I look at the boy I love, who loves me, more than I deserve. Who is so miserable loving me.

There is nothing left to say now, except,

305

Matthias, please leave.

He does not understand. I say it again:

Matthias, please leave.

He leans away from me and exhales deeply, looking out from the porch. Then, he turns his palms up and says:

Okay, Anna, whatever you say. We'll finish this conversation tomorrow.

He gets to his feet.

No.

He stops.

No what?

Do not come back tomorrow.

The look on his face. A full minute in stone, then:

You can't be serious, Anna.

I wish I were not, Matthias. But I can see it now, horribly in front of me: the future.

He will never leave. Not of his own accord. He loves me too much for that. He will come back night after night until I beat anorexia. But I will not beat it because I cannot. I cannot beat anorexia. I will not win and I love him too much to trap him in this future with me.

I say the horrible words a third time:

Matthias, please leave.

I cannot eat cream cheese on a bagel. Matthias, please leave.

I cannot eat the crêpes I make that you love. Matthias, please leave.

I cannot eat if I am sad or alone. I cannot eat in a restaurant. I cannot have the baby we wanted. Matthias, why are you still here?

Why are you still here?

I am not leaving, Anna. Where would I go if I did? There is no Matthias without Matthias and Anna.

But there is no Anna anymore.

67

My nasogastric feeding tube is a Capri lemon shade of yellow. It goes in through my nose, runs down my esophagus, and ends inside my stomach. Nutrition can be delivered through the tube in one large infusion, or gradually, via pump over a period of eight to twenty-four hours.

Or in the case of an evening snack, in ten minutes flat.

The procedure is surgically swift and lonely. It takes place in the nurse's station. The other girls cannot see me from the other room but I can hear their conversations.

I ask to use the bathroom. The humiliating sound of jingling keys. Perhaps it is the tube, or not, either way, I am choking for breath and in tears. I close and lock the bathroom door and let myself sink to the floor. Finally alone again, I cry.

Matthias is gone.

Matthias is gone. I sent him away. I know I did the right thing. At least now as I free-fall I know I will not be taking him down with me.

I keep the bathroom light switched off. I stay on the floor for hours. Or minutes, or a second,

I do not know. No one knocks for me to come out.

I finally stand up and switch the light on, reaching for the faucet. I jump: my reflection in the mirror. I look old, sick, and hideous. Scary. I switch the light back off.

But even in the darkness again, I cannot unsee my face, my body, the feeding tube. I look fat. I feel fat. Anorexia: there it is.

I dissect every body part outlined in the shadowy mirror. My breasts are far too small for the rest of me, and my legs are far too short. My behind sticks out more than it should. My thighs could and should be thinner. My back could be straighter, my shoulders more square. I could tuck my stomach further in.

Even my vision is distorted. *Macular thinning;* even eye muscles can lose weight, detect less detail, less light, send less dopamine to the brain. Life loses focus in the haze.

I hate what I see, even as my eyes squint in my self-imposed dusk. Shapes are hazy and disfigured, shadows look longer than they are, but the feeding tube glares directly at me, and Matthias is gone.

68

I leave the bathroom and go up the stairs, to the Van Gogh room. I do not bother to turn on the light. I climb straight into bed.

It is dark and quiet and not cold and under the covers, I could be anywhere. I pretend I am home and that Matthias will be next to me when I wake up.

Anorexia nervosa has been indisputably linked to other mood disorders, such as depression and anxiety. Some symptoms overlap and co-occur.

I hear the psychiatrist's voice in the report he wrote about me.

The patient may experience apathy, or indifference to her environment.

The next day I do not get out of bed. No vitals and weights for me today. Direct Care and the nurse warn, threaten me, but *no thank you.* I stay in bed.

Other symptoms include fatigue, loss of appetite and concentration.

Breakfast comes and goes without me. I do not get out of bed.

Pessimism and hopelessness.

They use my yellow tube. I let them. I am not allowed a morning walk, they say.

I do not care. I pull the covers back over my head and ask,

Just turn the lights off when you leave please, and close the door.

I am too tired for a walk.

Some time later the light is switched on again. I am mildly irritated. Direct Care says my father called.

Tell him I went to bed.

Matthias called too.

Tell him I went to bed. And please switch off the light.

One in five patients with anorexia will attempt suicide.

I know that statistic. I want to be one of them, but I am too tired to try. So I stay in bed. No reason to get up.

Matthias is gone. Direct Care finally turns off the light. I go to sleep.

69

Someone turns the light on. Again. Why? When?

Footsteps. Loud footsteps. Someone is angry. What day, what time is it?

Five thirty, Anna. Time for vitals and weights.

Emm is in the Van Gogh room. Emm pulls the covers back. Emm opens the window, the one we were expressly told to keep closed.

Emm opens my closet, searches for and finds the horrible flower-print robe. I look at her with mild curiosity. She throws the robe on the bed.

Put it on or I will make you.

She is already wearing hers. Her voice is low but its tone and her eyes make it clear that she is furious.

You have five minutes, Anna. Get dressed. I'll be downstairs.

She walks out. Leaving the light on and the door open, and me just starting to absorb this.

I take a few seconds to register what she did, then decide I do not care. I pull the covers back. The light can remain on, and the door open. She can wait downstairs.

Footsteps again, now very loud and angry. The covers are snatched away. Emm throws them to the floor. I want to protest, but I have no energy.

She grabs me by the arm and yanks me forward with surprising strength for an anorexic. To my utter horror she grabs my T-shirt and pulls it right over my head.

Ice-cold air. I shriek.

Good, so you are alive. Now you'd better listen to me.

She holds the flower-print robe beyond my reach. I wrap my arms around me, shivering.

Matthias did not come last night, but you already know that. Why didn't he come, Anna?

Because I told him not to come. She and I both know that.

You're an idiot,

she says.

Get up and bring him back.

I cannot believe what is happening. Cannot believe Emm is speaking to me like this. I am angry and cold.

Give me my robe!

Not a chance, Anna.

Leave me alone! Go away!

No, you had your day in bed! Now it's time for vitals and weights!

She does throw the robe in my face. I slip it on hurriedly, fuming. I feel naked and humiliated, cold and angry. I feel furious! I can feel something!

Get out of my room and out of my business! Who the hell do you think you are?

I'm the girl who's stopping you from making the biggest mistake of your life!

She is shaking too, and screaming, her wild hair all over her face.

Bring Matthias back! You have no right to give him up! You have no right, you have—

She chokes up.

Emm is crying and shaking with anger so violently she eclipses mine. Emm, mask down and composure in shreds. Emm is falling apart.

You have to bring him back,

she says jaggedly.

You have to win this one. You have no right to give up. If you can't, Anna, then what am I . . .

I cannot bear to watch her cry. I have never seen so much pain.

Naked underneath my horrible robe, I get out of bed. I hesitate before touching her, then I hug her. She does not push me back.

We stand there, two anorexics in horrid flowery patient robes, Emm's tears soaking mine and hers. She cries herself to a stop, then silence. When she pulls back she is calm. Her voice is steady as she says,

Let me explain a few things to you, Anna.

There is nothing left of the despair that ransacked her minutes before. Emm the cruise director is back.

315

I understand what you're going through. We all do, every girl here. And no, Matthias doesn't, but that doesn't mean that he is not suffering.

Her dispassionate tone clashes against the content of her words.

Matthias does not sleep at night because he is thinking of you. He worries about you in the morning, at work, on his way over here and when he leaves. He thinks about you when it's cold and windy and snowing outside. He thinks of you at every meal. He thinks about you in every restaurant he goes to, poring over the menu for one item he thinks you might eat.

The more she talks, the more my heart hurts.

You have someone who worries about you. Do you understand how lucky you are? Every girl here watches him come here every damn night for you and wishes someone came for her. And if you think sending him away will protect him in some weird twisted way, it won't. He'll just worry about you more. He loves you and you're hurting him. You have no right.

I am crying into my hands. *He loves you and you're hurting him.* I remember Julia calling me one of the lucky ones. *You have no right.* I think of Valerie.

Sarah, missing her little boy. Emm, who has been here for four years.

You don't have the right to send him away.

You don't have the right to give up. He's asking you to eat. Eat, dammit! He loves you! You're the luckiest girl here!

My eyes feel like they will burst. I look up at Emm. My voice is hoarse:

I do not know how.

In her business voice, she replies:

Well, you start by getting dressed. Vitals and weights, and then breakfast. Then keep going from there. Get that damn tube out of your nose. Get through your meals and snacks. And find a way to bring Matthias back.

I force my breaths calmer and longer and look at this girl saving my life.

Thank you, Emm.

Don't thank me. Do it. Now let's go downstairs. Come on, vitals and weights! We're late.

In our patient robes, mine wrapped at the front, we go downstairs together.

70

I am not allowed coffee, and breakfast is infused, but I am out of bed, dressed, and downstairs. I wait in community space while the other girls eat. At eight thirty, they stand up and disperse. Direct Care clears the dishes from the breakfast table and then comes to me.

Your therapist wants to see you at nine, and your treatment team at nine thirty.

The other girls go on the morning walk. I remain on the couch.

The house is quiet, till the sound of a car pulling into the driveway. Doors opening, closing, a suitcase being wheeled to the front of the house.

It cannot be a new admission. Today is not Monday. The front door opens and in walks the sickest, thinnest girl I have ever seen.

What first strikes me is her suitcase; it looks very much like mine. Blue. Her worried husband, who looks a little like Matthias, carries it inside. She is dressed as I would be: in layers. She looks sick, cold, and old. I try not to stare, but her face stops me like a heart attack. Her eyes, her nose, the thin line where her lips are supposed to be.

Danielle?

Direct Care shakes both strangers' hands. I hope she is gentle on hers. Even from a distance Danielle's frail wrist looks ready to break.

Please have a seat. I will be with you as soon as I take Anna to her team.

Danielle jars me more than every book and article on anorexia I ever read. More than the numbers on the scale, those on my test results. More than all the other girls I met here. Perhaps it is the suitcase. Or her husband. Or that she looks like me.

Perhaps it is the blatant truth that this woman is dying. Bones and blue fingernails; this is anorexia. It is hideous. I cannot stop staring.

Something else is bothering me, but I cannot put my finger on what it is.

Then I do. Then my insides turn cold and there is no more air in the room.

Anna, are you ready?

Today is not Monday. Admissions are on Mondays. And yet Danielle is here.

Anna, did you hear me?

I understand what Danielle means.

Valerie is dead.

Anna!

71

Direct Care has to take me by the arm to the office with the gray suede couch. The force of her grasp brings some of the feeling back. The therapist is already inside, waiting for me. I do not sit down.

Valerie is dead.

I wait.

She does not correct me. I needed her to. I needed her to! I panic.

What the hell am I doing here? *Valerie is dead.* My words echo horribly in my ears. How can the therapist just sit there and watch me? Why can I not scream?

I cannot scream because there is no air. Only my face in the mirror. And Valerie's. And Danielle's. And the thought: *We all look exactly the same.*

Anorexia is the same story told every time by a different girl. Her name does not matter; mine used to be Anna but anorexia got rid of that. And my feelings, body, husband, life. My story will end as Valerie's had.

Valerie is dead, and the therapist's silence.

I collapse on the couch, sobbing.

The therapist sits quietly on the couch next to me. I can smell her peony perfume. Her name is Katherine. She wears summer dresses. She is human too.

I cry for a few minutes or a year, then the room and my feelings go mute. I let myself sink backward into the gray suede. I have no voice or tears or energy.

Katherine looks at the nothingness with me, then she sits up straight.

Valerie made a choice,

she says.

Not to have anorexia, but to die. You have a choice too.

Anorexia or Anna. Anorexia or Anna, except

It is too late. I no longer know how to live without anorexia. I do not know who I am without it.

Well, we can find out.

I am too tired. I tell her I am too tired.

Yes I know, Anna. Valerie was tired too. This is an exhausting disease. But you got out of bed, didn't you? Why?

Because Emm made me.

Why else?

Because Matthias. Because Papa and Sophie. Because of what Julia said about me.

Why else?

Katherine repeats.

Because I have a reason: Matthias.

322

She nods and leans back next to me.

I do not have the right to give up. It is not fair to Valerie. Perhaps if she had had someone like Matthias she would still be alive.

She did not, and she is not, but I can still be. How had I told Matthias to leave? How had I gone to bed?

I have to bring Matthias back,

I tell Katherine. I have to fix this. If not for me, for Valerie, Emm, and every girl in that house, each one of them as deserving as I of a chance to live and be loved. I am not special. I am just lucky. The luckiest girl in the world. And happiness is a choice: I choose Matthias and Anna. I must bring Anna back.

My thoughts are interrupted by a knock on the door. It is already nine thirty. The rest of the team and Direct Care file in. They all sit down facing me.

I must speak before they do. I have no clue what to say, but the words come out to both their and my surprise:

I want to go on a date with Matthias.

Stunned silence. I clarify:

A therapeutic meal outing.

They exist in the patient manual.

They look at me like I am mad. I look at me the same way. This very meeting was convened because I had hidden cream cheese, refused to complete my meals, been intubated, run away, been returned, gone to sleep. I should be going nowhere but to a high-security psych ward. But I am not mad, not yet. I just have to explain that to them.

Please, let me explain.

I look to the stony faces for help. From Katherine, a nod to proceed. That is all I need.

There is a girl outside with a suitcase like mine. Her husband brought them both here. She is dying. I can see it. I have never seen anything so clearly. She is dying and I do not want to die like her or Valerie.

My words are not coherent but are the best I can do. I continue:

I know I made a mess. I was tired and suffocating and I am still tired and suffocating. But I cannot lose Matthias and I do not want to die. Please give me another chance.

No reaction or response. Perhaps it is too late. I want to cry. I try one last time:

I want to go on a date with my husband, please.

And then, I wait.

72

Direct Care pulls a patient manual from the shelves over Katherine's desk, bulky and identical to the one I was given on my first day. She opens it and flips through the sections to:

"The Stages of Residency at 17 Swann Street."

I remember those. She begins:

"Stabilization Stage: Patients admitted at this stage may or may not recognize their eating disorder is a problem, and may or may not experience a desire for recovery."

Not. Definitely not.

"During this stage the focus is on medical stabilization, nourishment, and hydration. Due to the intensive level of supervision necessary, patients at this stage are not eligible for therapeutic passes, outings, physical activity groups, or daily walks."

In other words, hell. Girls rarely come here at Stabilization Stage, and if they do, rarely stay. They are often just too close to death to be outside a hospital ward.

Excuse me, Anna is at Stage One,

Katherine interrupts. Direct Care replies testily:

Yes, I was getting there.

She gets there:

"Stage One: Patients at this stage still require a high level of medical monitoring, but not one as extensive as that of patients at Stabilization Stage. During this time the focus is on medical stabilization, normalizing eating behaviors, developing adaptive coping resources, and establishing a collaborative working alliance with the treatment team."

"Collaborative." The operative word.

"Patients at Stage One may go on one therapeutic pass per week. Meals are not allowed on passes—"

Unless she is at Stage Two.

I look at Katherine, surprised but grateful; she is actually intervening for me. She reaches for the manual:

May I?

Direct Care hands it over to her. Katherine reads:

"Stage Two: Patients have decided that they are ready and willing to work for recovery. They collaborate with their treatment team to develop a course of action for their treatment."

She pauses for a pointed look at me:

"Patients at this stage must be committed to exploring underlying issues that have contributed to the development of their disease. They must also present with increased honesty and accountability for their behaviors . . ."

I wince—

"... *urges, and thoughts. They are allowed two meal passes per week.*"

She does not read on and into Stage Three. Too far away, too surreal. But she does look at me and ask:

Do you think you're ready for Stage Two?

Have I decided that I am ready and willing to work for recovery? Can I be honest and accountable? Do I want to collaborate?

Well—

The nutritionist protests:

She has a feeding tube in!

She and I exchange dirty looks. The psychiatrist asks her:

How's her weight?

She shows him my chart.

Hmm . . .

Katherine addresses me:

Anna, you have not answered my question.

No I am not ready, but I can only go forward from here . . . or to a hospital ward.

I want to try, I have to. I have to bring Matthias back.

No further questions. I am told:

Anna, you may go now, thank you. Direct Care will take you back to community space while the team makes a decision.

Neither Danielle nor her husband is in community space when I return. I conclude he probably left and she is probably in orientation. The rest of the girls are out on the morning walk. I have some time to waste. I decide to write Danielle a welcome letter, like the one Valerie had written me.

Short, signed, and folded. I slip it in my pocket to give to her when she returns. *It's what we do here.* The girls return, the mailman, and preparations for midmorning snack.

I do not see Danielle in the morning, or as we cross the lawn for lunch. After it I ask Direct Care about her. She says:

She had to leave. Don't worry: she's stable now.

73

Treatment Plan Update—June 10, 2016

Weight: 89 lbs.
BMI: 15.3

Summary:

Treatment team has approved patient transition to Stage Two of residential treatment, with reservations by team nutritionist.

In light of low patient weight, behavior and mood, and the continued need for feeding by means of nasogastric tube, treatment team acknowledges the precocity of this transition. However, it highlights that this transition is **exceptional and probationary**, approved with the main purpose of allowing patient to go on a therapeutic meal outing with her spouse.

Treatment team feels reasonably confident that the benefits of the therapeutic meal outing outweigh potential risks of noncompliance and relapse at Stage Two. Maintenance of Stage Two status is contingent upon patient's full compliance with her assigned meal plan, all treatment activities, and the team's instructions.

Date, location, and meal plan of the therapeutic meal outing will be determined by the nutritionist. Nasogastric feeding tube will remain in place as a precautionary measure. Failure to complete any meal or snack prior to the outing will result in the immediate revocation of the permission.

Residential treatment remains necessary.

Treatment Objectives:

Complete a meal with spouse without resorting to eating-disorder behaviors or necessitating nasogastric feeding tube.

Alleviate symptoms of depression and motivate patient to resume work toward recovery.

Resume normal nutrition, restore weight. If needed, ensure nutrition through nasogastric tube feeding.

Monitor vitals. Monitor labs. Follow hormone levels.

Target caloric value: Maintain and secure at 2,700 calories until reevaluation.

74

I will have the pizza margherita,
Anna told the waiter.
I knew it!
Matthias triumphed.
Of course you will, you unpredictable one.
To his teasing, she deftly responded,
Do not be too cocky, *mon ami.*
And to the waiter:
The gentleman, I believe, will have the *tartuffo.*
Extra mushroom and truffle oil.

Matthias laughed and topped the order with two glasses of the house red.

It was Friday night, one of their earlier dates, but he had already known her forever. He was also beginning to suspect that he was in love with her.

We're in a rut!
he lamented.
Boring!
she exclaimed, her mouth twitching mischievously.
Before we know it, we will be finishing one another's sentences.
Drinking our coffee the same way!

he added.

Ah non! Never!

she gasped.

You drown yours in cream and sugar!

And yours is disgustingly black!

They both laughed. He reached for her hand across the table and looked at her. She was beautiful.

I like knowing these little things about you,

she admitted shyly.

I like knowing what side of the bed you sleep on and the way you smell in the morning. How you like your eggs and fold your socks.

He was in love with her.

I like knowing that about you too.

The wine and pizzas arrived.

So tell me, Matthias, why do you cut off the crust?

It's a useless filler; I'd rather save the space for more mushrooms,

he said.

The crust is my favorite part,

she answered.

Really? Ha! You can have all of mine.

He put the first piece onto her plate. She bit off the end and smiled:

Merci! But what will I give you in return?

Hmm, let me think, olives?

The waiter had placed a small bowl of green ones on the table.

C'est parfait! I hate olives. You can always have mine.

And you can always have my crust.

Now we really are boring!

she laughed.

I love you,

he replied, leaned over the table and kissed her, pizza on their lips and all.

75

It was a tradition: Friday nights were our date nights, even after we were married. Tired or not, we dressed nicely and went out to places with wine lists and dim lights. Those outings, of course, had grown more sporadic as my food repertoire had narrowed. Till they had become nonexistent. And then I had come here.

Now it is 6:22, Friday night, and we are getting ready for dinner, after which Matthias will not be visiting, for the third night in a row. Still no word from my treatment team, and an hour till I get my phone back.

The usual air of quiet pre-meal dread sits with us in community space, our stomachs and minds in knots. I think of Matthias and wonder what he is doing right now. Is he home? Does he have plans for dinner? With a friend? A girl? A date?

Matthias on a date with someone else. The thought hurts too much. I suppress it. *Bring Matthias back,* Emm had said this morning. Was it only this morning?

I think back to our Friday-night dates. I remember that pizza night; I was wearing a black lace dress and little pearls in my ears.

I had also, uncharacteristically, let my hair down; Matthias preferred it that way. He was in slim-fitting blue jeans that suited him perfectly, and to this day my favorite striped shirt. He had worn it just for me.

I remember feeling giddy; the wine had been good, as had the pizza I had ordered. I remember the thin crust, fresh tomato and basil leaves, the creamy dollops of mozzarella. They had dribbled on my fingers and down my chin. Matthias had not minded.

I do not remember the taste of the pizza, though. Anorexia wiped that bit of memory out. Another thing I will have to bring back, but one step at a time.

Anna, may I have a word with you? This will only take a minute.

And to the other patients, Direct Care says:

Start lining up for dinner, please.

She takes me to the side; never a good sign. I am in trouble, or . . .

Your treatment team has reached a decision about your meal outing.

And?

And?

She smiles:

And I must call your husband to inform him of his date with you on Sunday night.

I could jump. I could hug her. Of course, I do neither. She continues seriously:

Remember this is all probationary. Do you understand that, Anna? If the meal outing goes well then the team will consider making your Stage Two status permanent.

It has to go well. It has to go well. I have to make this date work.

The nutritionist will come in tomorrow morning to plan the meal with you.

76

So what will it be?
the nutritionist asks, cutting right to the chase.
It is Saturday morning. We are both in her office,
I on the edge of the plump red chair.

She looks less than thrilled to be in my
company. I understand; it is her day off. I try to
set aside the antipathy I have been cultivating
for her for weeks.

I will be civil.
An Italian restaurant,
I say and, as an afterthought,
Please.
And what will you order there?
she asks.
A pizza margherita,
says the girl I once was, before I have time to
stop her.
Two full slices, at least,
comes her verdict,
and the house salad with dressing as well.

Her eyes are on the clock. I keep mine on the
prize. This painful meeting is adjourned.

77

Matthias pulls up at 17 Swann Street at precisely 6:00 P.M. on Sunday. I have not seen him since that horrible Tuesday. My heart is pounding madly.

I am wearing my navy-blue dress and white ballet shoes, my hair down. My outfit clashes with the yellow of my feeding tube, but I am too nervous to care. Matthias turns the engine off but keeps the radio on. He steps out of the car, sharp in a white shirt, beige pants, his sunglasses on.

I cannot make out the expression on his face. The sun is in my eyes. I wait nervously at the door. He reaches the house.

For all of two seconds we face each other. His face is solemn and foreign. *He is still angry at me.* My heart sinks. He has every right to be.

Hello,

I say.

Hello.

Polite.

My eyes beg his silently.

Then, he smiles! A shy and sheepish grin. I fly off the porch into his arms.

He kisses me. We stop. I kiss him back, again and again, crying.

I am so sorry,

as I try to compensate for the days of kisses lost.

His smell, his hair. I missed him.

I missed you,

he says, then kisses me again.

Then, abruptly:

Let's get out of here.

Let's.

Doors slammed, windows down, music turned back up, we drive off immediately in our blue getaway car, my hand on his switching gears.

The two of us, just the two of us again, we are both quiet. There will be time, later, to talk. Now the sun is warming my cheeks and nose and the music is soft, and besides we already summed the last five days up:

I missed you.

This time I say it.

We arrive, Matthias and Anna. The Anna he married, I hope. The girl he took on a date to a pizzeria, a Friday night years ago.

I am scared. Anorexia has tagged along, and the tube on my face will not let me forget it. No turning back; we walk into the restaurant. It is lovely; Julia had recommended it, and the table by the window.

We are seated. *Sir, madam, the menus,* and with

them a side of fear. I glance at the table to my right: an older couple, two giant, cheesy pizzas. Two glasses of wine.

I focus on my breath. Matthias is looking at the options on the menu. He always does, I realize, though he orders the same thing every time.

The familiarity of that act, the Matthias I knew, sitting in front of me. I exhale. The Anna he married; I must keep her on hand. Our waitress arrives.

What would you like to order?

Two glasses of house wine, red of course. Then Matthias and she look at me:

Ladies first.

I know what I should order, what Anna always orders, and how this date should go. But I did not leave 17 Swann Street fast enough:

If I have the pizza marinara . . .

I begin. A little voice in my head continues: *then I could eat more bread.* I do love bread, and do not care much for mozzarella anyway.

That was not the plan,

Matthias begins uneasily.

The nutritionist said . . .

I look sharply at him, outraged that he and the nutritionist had spoken behind my back.

I know what I am doing. Please do not police me. I get enough of that back there.

No sooner have the words left my mouth than I regret saying them.

Matthias looks away from me and at his menu again. I can hear the silent thoughts in his head, even louder than the screams in mine:

Nothing has changed.

He is right.

The waitress looks down at her notepad. I want to defend myself, to explain, to her and him, the tube, the cheese, my heart beating so loud I am certain everyone around me can hear it.

A pizza marinara is not anorexia! pleads the voice in my head. I am not sick; I am a girl on a date who simply does not like mozzarella.

Then I hear it: my own lie. Two voices in my head: anorexia's and mine. Deep down I know which is ordering the pizza marinara.

I see the past four weeks go up in pale, translucent smoke, Valerie and the other pale translucent girls in their robes. My own robe in the Van Gogh room. My husband across from me. I see the years of Friday nights with him that I lost because I could not eat.

Never mind,

I tell the waitress. And my anorexia to be quiet.

I would like to start with a house salad please. Then a pizza margherita.

She writes the order down, unaware of its implications.

And what would you like, sir?

I eat the salad. And the dressing, and cheese. Then I eat my pizza. One slice of it, two.

Calmly cutting the pieces with my fork and knife, chewing, fighting my brain for every bite. I pause at times to sip at my wine, look at Matthias, look at us.

I finish, lay my silverware down, and my courage, and begin to cry.

Still not looking at me, Matthias finishes his last slice. He has eaten all of his pizza, extra mushrooms and truffle oil, and left the crusts on the side, because

Matthias ate the olives Anna did not like, and Anna always took his crust.

Matthias and Anna held hands across the dinner table, talked with their lips, their eyes, their feet. Anna and Matthias emptied bottles of wine together, shared ice cream cones and French fries. Anna peeled oranges for Matthias because he had never learned how. He ate the olives she did not like and always gave her his pizza crusts.

I reach across the table and touch his hand.

May I have a piece of pizza crust?

For a second he does not look up. His hand does not move. I am too late.

Then he gives me a piece and looks at me. He is crying too.

He talks.

About guilt. Toward me, toward Papa and Sophie, even Maman and Camil.

I promised your father when we got married

that I would take care of you. We came here and I promised you that you would not be lonely.

I am sorry I worked late. I am sorry you had to eat so many meals alone. I am sorry I did not say anything sooner, sorry I did not push harder.

That moment at the airport last Christmas, Anna. The look on your father's face. I had loved you too close to see what was happening. No, I chose what I wanted to see.

I look at this boy, this man who loved me, had married me not knowing what anorexia was. This boy who, in spite of it all, still loves me, is still sitting across from me.

I cannot love you and let you order your pizza without the cheese. I cannot love you and let you kill yourself.

I talk about guilt too, toward him.

For not being the wife he had married, not being what he had signed up for. For the empty bed in our apartment, this date and the others I ruined. Most of all, worst of all,

For not being pregnant. You deserve to be a father.

I choke.

We stop talking.

Matthias and Anna. Where had Matthias and Anna gone? We hold hands until we find them. Then we hold hands while we kiss with cheesy, salty lips and ask for the check.

While Matthias is away washing his hands,

the friendly waitress returns. She looks at me nervously.

I hope this is not too forward of me, but I understand what you are going through.

I am sure I have misheard. I look at her carefully. I have never seen her before. She looks like a girl who enjoys pizza, and life. Calm and comfortable in her skin. We could not be more unalike. How, what could she possibly understand?

17 Swann Street? I was there last year.

I am too stunned to speak. She shuffles her feet uncomfortably and continues:

I am much heavier now, and I probably look like your worst nightmare, but I am happy and I am alive. I would not give that, or the pounds, up for anything.

She clears a few crumbs off our table, I suppose to give her hands something to do.

I just wanted to tell you that I know it looks hopeless, and I know you want to die. But it gets better, I promise.

Then hurriedly,

Sorry to have bothered you. Good luck.

She walks away.

Matthias returns, pays the bill, and tips well. The service really was excellent. We drive back in the twilight, my hand on his switching gears. In the driveway, he kisses my hands and lips. I kiss him all over his face. I tell him we should have pizza again soon. And again, and again.

And I tell myself that perhaps I will enjoy it one day too.

Seven thirty, tomorrow night?

I ask.

Seven thirty. I'll be back.

And I will bring Anna back too, I promise Matthias in my head.

I wave the car goodbye, on the porch, thinking of all the girls who have lived here. The girls who really understand hunger, cold, and fleeting heartbeats. The Valeries and Danielles, but also those who are now waitresses, accountants, astronauts. Who go to movie theaters and theme parks, have babies and scones and lemonades on Sunday afternoons.

These strangers who no longer live here, these now not so invisible girls, looking after those who are still pale, still at risk of fading away.

78

The light is on in Julia's room. I pass it on my way to mine.

I wear my pajamas, the gray ones, and go back downstairs for bathroom access. Permission granted, I wash my face and scrub the taste of pizza out of my mouth. I wish I could do the same to the guilt in my head and stomach. Back upstairs, I sit on my bed, waiting for it to subside.

Julia's music is playing through our wall. I wonder if she is okay. I get off the bed. I want to thank her for recommending the restaurant anyway.

It takes a few knocks on the door of Bedroom 4 for the music to stop and Julia to come out. Her eyes are bloodshot from tears or something else. She is not okay.

She seems happy to see me, though:

Hey! You're back. How was the pizza?

Delicious. Thank you for the recommendation.

Anytime. They make the best pizza in town. I used to work shifts there; I should know.

She winks.

Did you get the window table?

Yes, we did.

Her face lights up.

Awesome! You were in Megan's zone. Was she on shift today?

So the waitress was called Megan. The sweet ex-anorexic who had understood.

She was wonderful,

I tell Julia.

She told me she had been a patient here.

Julia knows I have more to say and waits. I search for the appropriate words:

Dinner was . . . not easy.

No. Second try.

Dinner was extremely difficult. I am still not over it. But I did it.

Yeah you did!

She high-fives me then, still beaming, motions me inside. Amid piles of dirty laundry, books, records, and empty wrappers, we sit down on her floor.

Megan understands. That's why I wanted you to sit in her zone. I figured pizza would be hard tonight.

She was very patient with me. She really helped. Thank you so much, Julia.

She shrugs and smiles.

It's what we do.

Emm had said something similar.

It is my turn:

Are you okay?

Julia thinks for a moment.

No. No, I'm not. I haven't been for a while.

I give her space and time to talk, or not, if she wants.

Megan is the reason I came here, actually.

Really? How so?

She chuckles.

Well, working the same shift at a pizzeria, she and I discovered early on that we lived on opposite sides of the same problem.

Food?

We both wish it were as easy to sum up as that.

When you're fifteen and you love pizza, you eat pizza five dinners a week. When you move out of your parents' house and into a crowded dorm, you have it for breakfast the next day too. Pizza, my friend, is a remarkable cure for everything from hangover to heartbreak. Pizza replaces that 2:00 A.M. cramp in your stomach and mind nicely, with warm, salty, gooey lethargy. . . .

She pauses, presumably, to picture the pizza.

And then it's time for something sweet.

I can relate to the angst and the appeal of comfort food. I have spent my own share of time torturing myself in front of rows of crisps, crackers, and ice cream in supermarket aisles. The difference between Julia and me is that I cannot bring myself to eat them. The temporary comfort does not, in my mind, validate the guilty, nauseating knot in my stomach that follows. I ask her:

351

What were you anxious about?

Oh, nothing in particular at first, then every-thing, then nothing again. Uncertainty, I guess. Unfairness. Boredom, maybe? Pizza, ice cream, milkshakes, fries—they're reliable friends.

In a way, like hunger. At the other end, as Julia said, of this sad spectrum we are on. You cannot control your life, love, future, past, but you can choose what you put, or not, in your mouth.

College is hard,

she says. I agree. Like moving to a new city.

It wasn't at first, though,

she reflects,

I was on the coed basketball team. My team-mates and coach were the family I sweated, showered, and pigged out with. I wore workout clothes all the time and actually worked out. I never worried about what I ate. I was always relaxed, with myself and the boys.

Nonchalantly, she adds:

Until one of them raped me and, that same night, I discovered I could binge and purge.

There is nothing to say. I put my hand on her knee. She gives me her Julia smile.

Don't worry about me. It's fine. I'm fine.

It is not, nor is she. We both know that, but I do not want to interrupt.

Anyway, comfort food was comforting, but purging was a revelation. It solved so many problems, Anna. It drove the feelings out—like constantly hitting restart. Have you ever done it?

I have. Most anorexics do, at that breaking, starving point when the body turns on its brain and sets loose on carbohydrates, sugar, fat. Bread, berries, chips, lettuce, a raw onion or pickles in the fridge. Chocolate, cookies, cake, leftover food in the trash.

Then the tsunami of guilt, paralyzing. The rush to the toilet bowl. Fingers in, food out. Fingers in again. Speed is key, before the body can absorb any more nutrients and calories.

Yes, but rarely. Only when I lose control. The purging is punishment.

Interesting. For me, it's an addiction. That complete absence of energy and feeling, lying on the bathroom floor. I could stay there all day—and I did. All day every day for days.

She says it so casually.

It took up all my time. I dropped out of the team and out of college; I was too busy having double, triple breakfasts and raiding the supermarket. I was also exhausted and out of breath all the time. I lost my voice, got calluses, an ulcer. The palpitations sucked too, but money was my biggest problem.

Wry smile. Sad smile as she jokes:

Bulimia is an expensive habit. I stole from my mother and got the cleaning lady fired. I went through the dumpsters behind bakeries. I opened boxes of cereal and packs of cookies and ate them right in the store.

She stops to scrutinize me for signs of judgment. She finds none on my face—how could I—and continues:

*Then I got a job at the pizzeria and couldn't believe my luck: Free food! Free **pizza!** Endless amounts of it that people left on their plates! Yeah baby.*

She grins.

And there was Megan. We became really good friends. She would write orders down wrong on purpose so I could eat the pizzas that were sent back, and I would pick up her cleanup shifts so I could eat the leftovers.

She pauses. The thought crossing her mind at the moment does not seem very funny.

Then Megan had a seizure at work. I missed it—I was busy bingeing in the back room.

A week later, I got fired; apparently there's a fine line between digging into inventory and depleting it.

She chuckles at her own joke, then looks down at her fingernails. She seems quite engrossed by them.

Anyway she was at 17 Swann for a while, and I did not visit her. Now I'm the one who's here and she's out.

What made you finally come here?

Hypokalemia, actually. Bitch of a feeling, like a heart attack.

To my confused face, she explains:

It's when your potassium levels drop. It sucks. I collapsed a few months ago.

The levity in Julia's voice only makes her story more painful. I want to comfort this not-so-tough girl who is so kind and so brave, but she undercuts my good intentions in her signature light-humored way:

It's fine, I'm fine. I wound up here, sharing a wall with you, lucky one! Aren't you glad you live in Bedroom Five?

We both laugh. Very glad.

I stand up, bones crack. I walk toward the door.

She asks casually:

How are you feeling, really?

I answer with the same tone:

Horrible. Fat. Guilty.

Two wry smiles.

But it is all right,

I say.

I am going to sleep.

Sleep helps,

Julia says,

and if you find you can't, just remind yourself that there's coffee in the morning. Focus on that.

That's what Emm said.

79

Treatment Plan Update—June 13, 2016

Weight: 90 lbs.
BMI: 15.4

Summary:

Patient went on a successful meal outing with her spouse and has been completing her meal plan without recourse to nasogastric feeding tube. The treatment team interprets these developments as indicators of a shift in the patient's predisposition and motivation toward recovery. Consequently, team confirms patient's Stage Two level of treatment.

Conditional upon continued efforts toward recovery and compliance with the treatment plan, the team is not opposed to increased exposure to autonomous eating through more meal outings with spouse.

Residential treatment remains indicated, but nasogastric tube feeding is no longer necessary.

Treatment Objectives:
Resume normal nutrition, restore weight.

Remove nasogastric feeding tube.

Increase exposure to different foods. Encourage meal outings.

Monitor vitals. Monitor labs. Follow hormone levels. Monitor mood.

Target caloric value: 3,000 calories daily

80

Monday, and I have lost track of how many of those there have been. Time is a surreal concept that seems to have little place in this house. Dinner is done and visiting hours with Matthias are back. Matthias is back. I breathe out with relief as I reach for his outstretched hand.

We walk in the garden, in a circle around the house, my invisible leash acting as radius. One day I will grow up and step off the property where no one will tell me what to eat. Or how far to go, or what I may and may not do with my husband. My husband, hand in mine, walking beside me. I missed this, and us.

We do not talk about the week that passed. We talk about last night instead.

I had a lovely time, thank you.

I did too,

he replies.

A few steps later, he observes:

I hadn't seen you eat in a long time.

His voice is deliberately calm but a tremor sneaks in with the last word. I glance sideways at him, troubled:

Come on, Matthias—

I meant eat something that was not lettuce or an apple, or fucking popcorn.

He shuffles through his memories, then nods his head:

A long time.

His hand tenses in mine. We have stopped walking. He asks me abruptly:

You won't stop, will you? You won't give up again?

I cannot give him the answer he wants. Last week was too recent for that, and my throat is still sore from the tube that was only removed today.

I want to tell him: *I will not stop, Matthias.* That we will go on many more dates. Maybe even next Friday night. That I will have pizza again, or pasta next time. That next week I will be home, and that I will make crêpes for us both for dinner,

but time is as treacherous as it is surreal. So is an anorexic brain.

I tell him the truth instead:

I promise you that I will never stop trying.

It is not what he wants or deserves, but it is everything I have. He takes it:

All right, Anna.

One last lap around the house, then it is 9:00 P.M.

Evening snack, then exhale: the day is really over. I climb the stairs to the Van Gogh room.

And stop: there is a suitcase in the hallway, and new sheets and towels in Bedroom 3.

A new admission, but where is she? There had been no new face at evening snack. *Perhaps she arrived in the afternoon,* I reason, *and is still at orientation with Direct Care.*

I brush my teeth as fast as I can and disappear into Bedroom 5, closing the door and postponing introductions till tomorrow morning. I put on my pajamas and climb into Van Gogh's bed. A few minutes later I hear the floorboards creak and the door of Bedroom 3 close.

Well, I am already in bed. Besides, she must be tired. Surely the new girl does not want to be disturbed on her first night.

But I look up at the cracks in the ceiling I remember noticing on my own first night here. How lonely and scary, how long ago that first night had been. I had read Valerie's note to exhaustion. It is still on my bedside table. I look at my name in her cursive handwriting, and:

I'm so glad you are here. . . .

I pull the covers back and turn the night-light on. I need a paper and pen.

Dear neighbor in Bedroom 3,

Welcome to 17 Swann Street. I am glad you are here.

Do not let this place scare you. It is not as impossible as it seems.

I think of what else I can tell this girl, what else could help. Oh yes:

They serve good coffee in the morning that is well worth getting out of bed for. You get two cups, which is lovely. As is the morning walk. Once you are cleared to go on that you will meet Gerald, the dog.

And staff. She needs to know about staff:

The staff here is very nice. The nurse on shift tonight is particularly lovely. She has blue eyes. You will meet her in the morning when she takes your vitals and weight. The rest of the girls, you will meet over breakfast. They are all incredible. They will help.

Which reminds me:

We have a few house rules besides those you heard at orientation.

I open Valerie's note for guidance, and in my finest, most cursive handwriting begin:

All girls are to be patient with one another.

No girl left at the table alone.

Composure is to be maintained in front of any guests to the house.

Horoscopes are to be read and taken seriously every morning over breakfast.

Copies of the daily word jumbles are to be distributed then too. Responsibility for that falls upon the group leader, who will disclose the answers no sooner than evening snack later that day.

Note writing and passing is encouraged. No note must fall in Direct Care's hands.

Books, music, letter paper, postage stamps, and flowers received are to be shared.

The availability of cottage cheese in the house is to be celebrated every Tuesday, as are animal crackers, the morning walks, and any excursions on Saturday.

No girl will ever judge, tell on, or cause any suffering to the rest.

I end, rather lamely:

I really hope this helps.

By the way, my name is Anna. I hope we become good friends.

Letter folded, slippers on, I tiptoe to Bedroom 3 and slip it under the closed door.

A few hours later, I see the new girl sitting at the breakfast table. She has survived her first night, and has a cup of steaming hot coffee in front of her. I introduce myself and do not mention the letter. She smiles and does the same.

The coffee is good and strong this morning. Everyone has two cups.

81

Treatment Plan Update—June 17, 2016

Weight: 93 lbs.
BMI: 16

Summary:

Patient has been cooperating with the treatment team and been fully compliant with her meal plan since removal of nasogastric feeding tube on June 13. She continues to struggle with food types and quantities, but has been working on containing eating-disorder urges and negative thoughts regarding body image. Her weight continues to restore slowly, but the team is pleased with her progress and absence of associated complications.

The team will continue to work on weight restoration and increased exposure to food. Because patient's weight remains below 85% of team target, residential treatment remains indicated. Further caloric increases are also recommended.

Treatment Objectives:

Resume normal nutrition, restore weight. Increase exposure to different foods and work to decrease anxiety.

Monitor vitals. Monitor labs. Follow hormone levels. Monitor mood.

Target caloric value: 3,500 calories daily

82

Sunday again, but this is no ordinary Sunday on Swann Street. At the breakfast table, everyone is fidgety. Even, especially, Direct Care.

It is Family Day, an event the center organizes every few months. As Emm explained, loved ones are invited to come and spend the day, take part in meals, sessions, and activities with the patients and learn about eating disorders. Staff is available to provide information and answer questions about different therapies and treatment plans, as well as general guidance on how to deal with, well, us.

I thought it a very good idea, this Introduction to Eating Disorders course. Not that there is anyone I could have invited today; my family is an ocean away, and Matthias has already spent way too many visiting hours here.

Enthusiastic nonetheless about this out-of-the-ordinary day, I look around the table and wonder whose family members might be attending. Direct Care asks the question for me:

So, ladies, who's coming?

One of the girls, Chloe, says her daughters are. Julia is excited too: after three months here, she announces, her parents are finally going to visit!

Another patient's husband will also attend, and

What about you, Sarah?

No, darling.

Her red locks shake loosely.

I tried to get that no-good husband of mine to bring my son, but he won't.

I am sorry,

I tell her. She shrugs proudly and smiles.

It's all right. Probably best if little Charlie doesn't see me in a place like this anyway.

Direct Care turns to Emm and asks:

Did you invite her this time?

I do not know who *she* is but Emm says:

No,

with her plastic cruise director smile.

The minute hand on the clock passes the eight-thirty mark. The breakfast dishes are cleared. We are sent off to community space and informed that we are to behave. There will be no morning walk or church pass on this exceptional day. I frown, beginning to have reservations about Family Day.

At nine o'clock the doorbell rings and Julia rushes past us to the door. In the doorway stands a tall, lanky man in a suit.

Paul!

calls the new patient. Husband and wife hug

each other awkwardly under our curious gazes. She then walks him to a corner in community space and we all turn back to the front door.

The doorbell rings again. This time behind it stand a bespectacled man, flustered, and three girls. The eldest, I guess, is around thirteen. The youngest cannot be older than three. I recognize their faces from the photographs Chloe passed around this morning.

Chloe! Your family is here!

The girls hug their mother and are bashful . . . for a minute. Then they launch, with Chloe, into a rowdy game of hide-and-seek.

There are children in the house. There are children in the house! Screams and squeals and laughter too! Never have I been more grateful for chaos at 17 Swann Street.

The door again. Julia's parents, perhaps? I volunteer to find out.

At first I see nothing, then I look down: a giant bouquet of flowers! Bright violets streaked with lemon yellows, fiery orange shoots that look like flames, rare orchids and lilies in shades of deep mauve, blue, and red . . . all held by two little hands. Those belong to a little boy well concealed behind flowers and leaves. I know who he is instantly; he has Sarah's eyes. Her nose and freckles and heart-shaped face too, but his hair is a deep chocolate brown.

The toddler is far too intimidated and little

369

for me to remain towering over him, so I step out onto the porch and bend down to his level, peeking at him through the leaves.

Hello, my friend, what is your name?
Charlie,
comes the reply.
What beautiful flowers you have, Charlie! Which lucky lady are they for?

Charlie has no time to answer; he has been swept off his feet, flowers and all, by a tsunami of fiery red hair and lipstick in a flowery print dress. It had taken Sarah a minute to register her son's presence at the front door, then every motherly instinct she had been holding back since she arrived here had erupted.

She is larger than life. *An artist in every sense,* I think as I watch her hug her son. She cries and smiles and kisses him on the eyes, the forehead, the cheeks. She kisses every freckle on his nose. When he is finally released long enough to breathe the little boy says:

I got you flowers, Mommy.
What gorgeous flowers!
she exclaims as she takes them from his tired hands. The bouquet is nearly as tall and, I suspect, as heavy as he is.

All my favorite colors are here! Did you choose them yourself?
He nods timidly and replies:
I told Daddy you liked rainbow.

Where is Daddy? I wonder as I look beyond the porch. Magical as they are, surely the two-year-old and his rainbow bouquet did not arrive here on their own. Still, there is no Daddy in sight. When questioned, little Charlie replies:

He says he has to work and that he will come back to pick me up.

Sarah does not seem too distraught.

Our Family Day begins, and what a splendid, sunny day it is. For one day, 17 Swann Street is just a regular house. We still attend therapy groups, but in them we play games and draw pictures of our families and homes. We have our meals in the house next door, on the same clear plates wrapped in plastic, but I cannot possibly fear my cake with one of Chloe's daughters going *Mmm mmm,* making a frosting mess, licking her fingers and smacking her lips.

After lunch, we have music therapy outdoors, on pillows and rugs spread on the grass. Sarah brings crayons and paper from the sunroom so that she and Charlie can color. I watch her sketch two, three, four versions of a violet, orange, blue, and red bouquet. Charlie contributes, scribbling here and there with the crayons he holds clumsily in a fist.

It is a beautiful Sunday. Like all beautiful days, it goes by too fast. Five o'clock comes and we take the pillows and rugs back inside.

The grown-up goodbyes are civilized. Those to the children are teary. All too quickly the house at 17 Swann Street turns quiet again.

The girls are back in community space, but many of them are missing. Julia, and Sarah.

Has anyone seen—

I see Sarah in the next room, at the table.

She is looking at Charlie's bouquet and the three drawings of it that she made. I pull a chair close to her and sit down. I do not have anything useful to say.

She breaks the silence first:

Aren't the flowers gorgeous? Isn't my son gorgeous?

They are, and so is he.

You have a beautiful boy. He looks like you.

She beams at the compliment.

He's grown so big!

No sunglasses to shield her eyes, I see Sarah cry.

I do not know how to comfort a mother who is missing her son. I do my best: I put my hand on hers.

You have a reason to fight this disease. Charlie needs you. You have somewhere to be outside of here.

She nods and wipes mascara from the corner of her eyes.

I help her hang the four sketches of the bouquet on the wall in community space. The doorbell rings again. We stop. We look at each other, confused.

Family Day is over, and Matthias never comes before 7:30 P.M. So who is at the door at 6:05? Have we missed anyone?

83

I cannot believe it. I do not dare. Next to Matthias,

Papa!

I leap toward him, hanging on to his neck, terrified he may disappear.

What are you doing here?

Well, I was told it was Family Day. . . .

begins the story of how my father took two planes from Paris to see me.

I cannot stop hugging him. I do not let go. He smells of eau de cologne and every happy memory of my childhood.

Papa! Papa is really here! I am crying like a child, wrinkling his shirt, hugging him tighter. He holds me close to him, not letting go either.

Anna, Anna,

a small tremor in his voice. His hand ruffles my hair. He finally pulls back and hands me a cotton handkerchief.

You still carry those.

I laugh as I inelegantly blow my nose.

Of course.

He smiles, his composure back in place but his voice still shaky.

My father, his eau de cologne, and his hand-kerchiefs are here at 17 Swann Street. My heart could fly right out of my chest, I am so happy.

Only for the evening, though. I am very sorry, Anna. I was supposed to land yesterday but I missed my connection, and tomorrow I must be at work.

Only an evening. *Only* an evening? A whole evening with my father! I stare, overwhelmed, at this man who crossed an ocean for an evening with me.

And . . .

Matthias adds,

I have news that is good and bad. Your team has allowed you to go out.

Away from Swann Street with Matthias and Papa!

. . . but it will have to be a meal outing.

I understand. It makes sense; I will be skipping dinner here. But:

At least that way you get more time with your father, right?

Matthias adds hopefully.

Matthias, wonderful Matthias.

Yes!

I let go of Papa long enough to kiss my husband passionately.

Thank you,

I whisper, then step back to contemplate the two men of my life. I exhale the breath I have been holding in, but the pressure on my chest is still immense.

It is happiness; I could burst with happiness.

I love you,

to both of them.

Before we go to dinner, Papa requests a tour of 17 Swann Street. All I want is to leave; he and this place represent two worlds I never want to intersect. Nonetheless, I show him around. Ground floor: community space.

Good evening, ladies,

he greets the girls politely, with only the faintest accent.

I am Anna's father.

Good evening, MONsieur,

Direct Care answers formally. Irrepressibly, hilariously American.

Good evening, sir,

Emm says, a tad more composed, speaking on behalf of the group.

My name is Emm.

Ah! Yes, she told me all about you. It is a pleasure to meet you, Miss Emm.

He turns to me:

Yes, I see what you mean: she does look like Sophie.

Emm raises an eyebrow at me, but I have no time to explain, because,

And who is Valerie?

Papa asks next. I freeze. I had not told him.

Of course I had not told my father that Valerie had died. One does not tell one's family these things. Another rule at 17 Swann Street.

Sarah saves the day:

I am Sarah. Has Anna told you about me?

Oui bien sur! *The actress,* non*? Tell me, how is your son?*

Sorry to interrupt, Papa, but we have to leave soon.

Hurriedly, I sweep him out of community space, through the breakfast area, the sunroom, and up the stairs to my room.

Just as you described it,

he says.

My father in the Van Gogh room. He looks out of my window, admiring the setting sun and

that magnolia tree is lovely.

He sees the board and his picture on it alongside Leopold, Sophie . . .

She misses you, you know.

I wrote her and I tried to call, but she has not been answering me.

He sighs.

This is difficult for her to understand. It is difficult for me too.

My sister smiles brightly at me from the photograph. She looks happy, beautiful, healthy. Next to her, I look healthy too; that photograph is so old. We have the same eyes and the same heart-shaped face. We once shared a bedroom and clothes. I do not know when, where, or how we diverged to end up in such different places.

She will come around. I think she just needs time. She feels like she lost you,

her sister, who once loved cake, to anorexia and a house full of skeletal girls. I really hope Papa is right and Sophie will call. I miss her terribly.

We walk out and down the stairs, through the rooms again; he does not comment on the locked cabinets and bathroom doors.

It was lovely to meet you, ladies. Have a good evening,

he says to the girls before we walk out. The lifeless group waves us goodbye. We cannot reach the door fast enough.

Anna! Wait!

Direct Care. Now what? She puffs over, paper in hand.

Your meal plan for dinner tonight at the restaurant. The nutritionist left clear instructions.

She goes over those, three times, with me, while the minutes tick away and I fidget. My father and Matthias look away studiously, trying not to listen.

Is this clear, Anna?

Crystal. Good night!

Have a good time, and don't forget—

But I am already skipping off to the car with my father and husband.

84

We drive off and far, far away from number 17, Matthias behind the wheel, Papa to his right, I between them both in the back seat. It is a blissful ride. We talk of random things, the conversation flowing as though we had last seen each other just this morning.

I look at Papa; he had been crying the last time I had really seen him. Now his forehead seems less tense, his hand reaching over his shoulder for mine, his jetlagged eyes closed, his head swaying softly to the song on the radio. It had been Christmas last time.

Matthias too, seems more relaxed; from where I sit I can tell from his shoulders. In Paris they had been stiff and high, now they are loose. He leans back.

Papa, how is Leopold?

As cheeky as ever, but I think he is getting old. Lately he has been letting me win when we run up the stairs to the flat. What about that dog you see on your morning walks? What was his name?

Gerald.

She told you about Gerald?

Matthias asks, amused.

Naturally.

Papa winks at me through the mirror.

We reach the restaurant Matthias chose, a tiny affair of a place. Eight tables at most, and utterly charming. Our table for three is the one by the window, under the chandelier.

We order three glasses of prosecco, to start. I kiss Matthias:

This is beautiful. Thank you.

Then:

To the men in my life, and how lucky I am.

It is a gorgeous evening. The waiter arrives:

What would you like to have?

I pull out my menu and my good intentions to comply with my meal plan. I give myself a few seconds to breathe while the waiter goes over the specials.

I know what to order; the instructions are clear and folded neatly in my purse. Papa and Matthias are waiting, I know, for a glimpse of the Anna they remember. This is my chance to show them both how far I have come, how cured I am. My chance to bring Anna back. All this hard work,

but I panic. Instead,

I order a side salad. Matthias sighs. Silence. Breath,

and the ratatouille.

There!

My father and husband nearly fall off their seats. I genuinely laugh out loud.

Papa says:

I will have the same. I have not had ratatouille in years!

Make that three then, with three side salads please,

Matthias tells the waiter. Menus shut.

We do not order appetizers, but all three of us dig into the bread. Papa and Matthias spread freshly creamed butter on theirs. I am not quite that cured yet.

Our salads arrive, and our main dishes are steaming hot, well seasoned, excellent. The conversation is mild but pleasant. Papa leads it, thankfully. He and Matthias do most of the talking while I focus on bite after bite. *Just as we practiced at 17 Swann Street,* I nudge myself on.

I am the last to finish, but I do finish. Fork down, I reach for my glass. A celebratory sip of prosecco; now I can concentrate on Papa's story. Matthias is listening to him intently, but underneath the table, his hand reaches for mine and squeezes it proudly, then remains on my knee.

Lady and gentlemen, would you care for dessert?

Papa looks at me expectantly. He will follow my lead. I check in with my anxiety: the old Anna would have ordered dessert in a heartbeat.

I suppose we could have a look at the menu,

I say to buy myself some more time. A decision

I regret: chocolate fondant, *crème brûlée, tarte aux framboises, au citron*, profiteroles . . .

The foreign voice in my head, panicked and jumpy, wants to say

No thank you. Check please.

The real Anna would have ordered dessert: the chocolate fondant with three spoons. Papa's favorite, and Matthias loves chocolate too. But I am no longer she. I am an anorexic fraud whose place is at 17 Swann Street. Who am I fooling with my glass of prosecco, my ratatouille, my bread?

Matthias, Papa, and the waiter are still waiting for me to reply. Guessing my answer, breaking the silence, Matthias asks for the check.

I feel like crying. Like I let them both down, especially Papa. Papa, who crossed the globe to be here with me only for a night. And even for a night, I cannot order dessert, cannot keep up a simple pretense. Cannot fight anorexia for another hour, just another hour, for him.

Can't I?

Big breath. Quick, before I have time to think:

I know where we can get dessert.

I laugh for the second time this evening at the expression on both faces.

We have ice cream, of course. Vanilla for me, chocolate strawberry for Matthias. And for my father, two large scoops of chocolate, with chocolate sprinkles *and* chocolate sauce!

Would you like some sprinkles, Anna?
Of course, Papa, but rainbow ones.

I watch them melt into blue, red, orange, and green swirls in the creamy white.

Anna used to love the colored sprinkles when she was a child,

Papa informs Matthias.

Yes she did, Papa, and she is still the Anna you remember.

We eat in the car, windows down, in the parking lot by the kiosk. There are a few other cars; a few couples, a group of teenagers. Trying perhaps, like us, to lengthen the last few minutes of Sunday.

We finish our ice cream with ten minutes to spare before we have to head back. I ate the little, but whole, scoop. And the sprinkles, and the little cone. Matthias says,

I am very proud of you.

I look at him gratefully; he had heard my anorexia screaming tonight, had watched me fight it silently, and had silently cheered me on. Matthias is proud of me.

As am I,

says Papa.

And amazed at how far you have come. Keep walking, Anna. Don't stop.

Keep walking, Anna.

He used to say that to me when I was little. When my feet hurt and blistered, when I scraped my knee, when I was tired on a hike. *Keep walking,* when it rained. *Keep walking,* when I was teased in the playground, called in the street, when I fell.

Dust off your knees, get back up. Keep walking, Anna. As he and Maman had done together, as he had then done alone. As he still did every morning with Leopold, every afternoon with me on the phone.

I am scared, Papa.

I know you are.

This is so difficult. It hurts.

I know, Anna. Life does, and it is messy.

You never told me that.

No,

he acknowledges.

I did not know it either, until your mother and brother. Just as I did not know what anorexia was until last Christmas.

He looks onto the parking lot, now empty. The ice cream kiosk is closed.

There is no tragedy to suffering. It is, just as happiness is. To be present for both, that is life, I think. And it is a beautiful evening.

It is, and I am here to witness it with the two men of my life. I am grateful, for it and for the long painful walk that brought me here.

I am not ready to die. I want more evenings like this, more time with him. With Matthias, with Sophie, with a baby. I want the happiness,

I will take the sadness. *Keep walking.* All right, Papa.

The ten minutes end. We roll up the windows and drive back to Swann Street. At number 17, Matthias slows, turns, parks. The last few seconds in the car, silently.

Papa and I step out. I hug him one last time, breathing in the familiar cologne. Then he gets back into the passenger seat and they leave for the airport.

I wave my father and husband goodbye, the Anna they knew till the end, then Matthias's blue car turns onto the street and out of sight. I am tired. I sit down.

My name is Anna, and I have a life and people who love me waiting outside 17 Swann Street.

I have a husband, a father, a sister, a reason to keep walking. It is a beautiful evening. I spend one more minute in it, then stand up and go inside.

85

Hours after evening snack has been distributed, consumed, and cleared away, I lie on my back in the Van Gogh room. I have a stomachache. Perhaps it is the ice cream, the ratatouille, or the snack, or the gaping void my father left. I sit up in bed and turn the night-light on. My watch says 3:43.

I give up on sleep and get out of bed and into a soft sweater and slippers. Then I tiptoe downstairs for a glass of water. Any excuse to leave the room.

The house is deathly quiet, except for the light snores coming from the nurse's station. The nurse has about an hour and thirty minutes left before vitals and weights. Direct Care is in there too, asleep, in an uncomfortable position on a chair. I must not wake them up. I head to the breakfast area but stop when I see the light on in the living room.

I peek in to find Emm curled up in the brown leather armchair in the corner. Her wild and curly hair is up for the night. Her cruise director mask is off.

She looks tired. Not the sleepy kind. She asks flatly:

What do you want?

Nothing. A glass of water. Do you want one?

No. Actually, yes.

Two tap waters come right up. I hand her one and stand in the doorway uncomfortably with mine.

How did your dinner go?

she surprises me by asking. The question itself is innocent, but the tone of her voice makes me wary. I opt for a cautious answer:

Very well, thank you. How was yours?

handing the reins back to her.

Do I really look like your sister?

she asks. My insides cringe.

No turning back.

I did tell my father that.

What is your sister like?

I am uneasy with this conversation but cannot avoid it. I answer:

Very different from me. She does not have an eating disorder.

Neither does mine.

You have a sister?

A twin.

Emm had never mentioned a twin. Emm had never mentioned her family. In fact, Emm never spoke of anything personal besides *Friends* and the Olympics, really.

Was she the person Direct Care was referring to this morning? Was she supposed to come to Family Day?

Yes. And no, because I didn't tell her.

She turns the tables on me:

Are you and your sister close?

Sophie and I used to be, but when anorexia happened we drifted apart. We have not spoken since Christmas.

My twin and I haven't in years. Not since my first stint here. She actually came to my first Family Day.

Then what happened?

Nothing. She left.

Her voice is misleadingly nonchalant.

She left, and I stayed. Then I was discharged. Then I relapsed and returned here. She came to the second Family Day, but not the third.

Then I stopped answering her calls. I had nothing interesting to say. She was calling less and less anyway. I don't blame her,

Emm says.

Her life was moving on. Mine was not.

I think of Sophie and everything I do not know about her life now. I wonder if she has a boyfriend. If she still likes her work, and cake.

Emm's features, in front of me, have hardened, but I know it is just for show. She *is* a lot like Sophie; Sophie's jaw clenches like that when she is trying not to cry.

I want Emm to continue but am scared to push her too far. I decide to wait. A few minutes later she regains composure and speaks:

We cut off all contact after our birthday three years ago. I had just been discharged, again. Just in time for the party actually.

What happened?

I couldn't eat the cake. The icing was pure sugar and food coloring. I couldn't—or wouldn't, my twin said—eat most of the food that was there. She said I made her feel guilty when she did, and that I wasn't trying hard enough.

She pauses.

I guess she just got tired of anorexia and waiting for me to fix it.

But you cannot "fix" anorexia.

I know,

she answers tiredly.

Four years in and I'm still trying to.

We sit together in silence.

I break it this time:

What is your sister's name?

Amy,

she replies. Then repeats it, lower:

Amy.

Her cruise director voice returns:

Perhaps it is better this way.

What is?

That she and I don't talk. At least I know she won't develop anorexia one day because of me.

Even I know it does not work that way.

You cannot pass anorexia to your sister.

No, but she could copy me.

Emm, it's a disease.

But Emm is not listening:

I couldn't bear it if she ended up here.

I could not bear it either, the thought of Sophie at 17 Swann Street.

Your sister is a grown-up,

I tell Emm.

You are not responsible for her.

She disagrees:

You are responsible for those you choose to love.

86

We hear a loud crack, a plate crash, an injured scream in the kitchen. Both Emm and I freeze. Running footsteps, a struggle, one, two voices screaming. The first we recognize as Julia's:

I was just getting a snack! I was hungry! What kind of sick place locks food away?

More footsteps. The night nurse has come in and is trying to pin her down.

Fucking let go of me! I want to leave! You can't tell me what to eat and do! I'm sick of these rules! Let me go!

Her screams are shrill and desperate, ricocheting off the house's walls. Julia is suffocating. I put my face in my hands and whisper, *Please, just let Julia go.*

I can leave when I want! Let go of me, dammit! I want to go home!

The screams turn to sobs, to pleas. I am crying too. I do not want to picture Julia, happy carefree Julia, pinned down.

For a snack. *Just a snack!* What a duplicitous disease. We all know it was a binge. Even Julia, though she keeps screaming:

I just wanted a snack! Let go of me, bitch!

Julia's parents had not come to Family Day. They had not even called. And none of us had noticed, I realize now. She had not brought it up. In fact, she had feigned studied indifference, breezing through the afternoon, dinner, evening. She had made it all the way to her room, I suppose, before falling apart.

Julia's voice is muffled. She gradually calms down, probably as the shot of Haldol begins to take effect. Emm and I stay in our spots, frozen quiet, while we hear some feet shuffle away. The nurse carries her up to bed while Direct Care cleans the mess.

Julia had been alone in her room while I had been out with Papa. She had been fighting her demons while I had been having ice cream with sprinkles.

I could have been there when she needed me, but I had been downstairs with Emm. Perhaps she had knocked on my door. We could have talked, and perhaps it would have helped.

Emm and I sit in the living room, she on the leather armchair, I on the couch. The house is quiet again. Eventually Direct Care finds us.

What are you doing here?! Go to your rooms and to sleep, you two! You barely have half an hour left before vitals and weights.

I go upstairs. Julia's door is closed. It still is half an hour later. She does not emerge for vitals, weights, coffee, or the jumbles at breakfast. The latter begins promptly at 8:00 A.M. and ends at 8:30 sharp. We go on our walk. When we return we are informed that Julia has been discharged.

I run upstairs. Yes, her room is empty. Painfully, whitewashed empty. Not a vinyl, piece of chewing gum, or empty wrapper. No sock forgotten under the bed. Like Valerie, not a trace of Julia left. Another disappearing act, like a punch in the gut. The vanishing girls of Swann Street.

You know the rules, Anna,

Direct Care's voice says. She is standing behind me.

You should not be up here after breakfast.

Where did you send Julia?

My voice is far too high-pitched.

She touches my shoulder lightly. I pull back, scalded.

How could you send her away?

Direct Care wants to calm me down, but knows better than to touch me again.

She assaulted a staff member.

She did not mean to!

I know, Anna, but those are the rules. She posed a serious threat to the patients and staff—

Julia would never hurt anyone!

Anna!

Direct Care is no longer patient. Her next sentence bites:

She knew the rules. She broke them.

She is sick!

So is every patient here.

Her cynicism slaps at my face. For once I really look at Direct Care: she is tired, and old, much older than I realized. Direct Care is her job, not her name. And Julia in her notes today will be: *Discharged Patient from Bedroom 4.*

But I am not jaded yet. Julia is still Julia to me: my friend, and

Julia cannot leave!

She cannot give up! is what I mean.

You will bring her back,

you will help her,

won't you?

Now my voice is low, begging.

She does not reply. I know she cannot. I try again nonetheless:

Will Julia be okay?

Direct Care sighs.

I really hope so.

87

On Mondays the day and night staff switch shifts, new admissions are brought in. The schedule starts over, and so do the meals. I know this by now; this is my fifth.

Monday morning also means a debrief of my weekend successively with the therapist, the nutritionist, the psychiatrist. Their own weekends they spend away from eating disorders and 17 Swann Street. They probably have brunch, cocktails, go to yoga classes or on runs. Not that they speak of those with us.

My session with Katherine is scheduled, as usual, post–midmorning snack, at ten thirty. That meal is particularly rushed today; I was delayed by the Julia affair. At least it is incident-free; I am used to the yogurt at this point. I sprinkle granola and swirl it into the vanilla. Both no longer scare me. Too much.

Ready, Anna?

Last bite, then yes. Direct Care checks my empty bowls and nods. Then walks me to the now-familiar office. I take my usual place on the couch.

Katherine comes in.

How was your weekend, Anna?

This time I am ready for her.

It was actually wonderful.

I tell her, in detail, about the evening I spent with my father.

She hears me talk about dinner and dessert. Asks:

How did the ice cream taste?

Painful, but worth it. You should have seen the look on my father's face when I ate it.

So you would have it again?

A loaded question. I contemplate it and the window.

Yes, if it means that I get another evening like this with him.

She looks up from her intensive note taking to smile genuinely at me. For a second, Katherine the therapist disappears and Katherine, just Katherine, says:

You may get more than an evening, Anna. You may just get your life back.

But she seals that crack swiftly and her next question is professional again:

Would you say you want recovery now?

Another loaded question. I balk. Rather, part of me does, clinging to the safety of the anorexia I know. The other part answers:

I would say I want to try.

At what cost?

She pushes,

Dairy? Protein, fats, and sugar? Eating those every day?

She leans forward and asks:

Anna, do you think you are ready for Stage Three?

Silence. In my head too. I have no idea what Stage Three entails. I tread cautiously:

What exactly does that mean?

Katherine reaches for the patient manual, flips it open, and reads:

"Stage Three: Patients at this stage still require daily medical monitoring and treatment for their eating disorder, but have demonstrated their commitment to their recovery and collaborating with their treatment team. They have experimented with instances of limited autonomy and exposure to eating-disorder triggers, and have performed satisfactorily."

I suppose both meal outings were experiments, and my performance was satisfactory.

"The focus is now on a protracted and gradual increase of patient autonomy and exposure to normal life circumstances—"

How so?

I interrupt.

"By downgrading treatment and supervision to ten hours daily."

Meaning?

She looks up at me and translates:

Meaning you would still have to come in for

full treatment programming every day, eight to six, but would no longer be required to have dinner or sleep here.

The air and thoughts race through my brain as it registers that last sentence. I am surprised at my first reaction: *No, I am not ready for Stage Three.*

I have only been on two meal outings. I had one ice cream cone, once! Forcing myself to eat dinner, every day, unsupervised, on my own?

No.

Her professional face does not stand up to this. Katherine is genuinely shocked:

What do you mean no, Anna?

No I am not ready.

But I thought you said—

What I said is irrelevant! Now I am panicking.

I do not know how I managed it! It was just an outing with Papa! I cannot do this every day—

But don't you want to?

The softness of her tone nips the anxiety in the bud. She lets the question float. I contemplate it, and the image of me having a meal on my own. She looks back at the manual:

"Patients at Stage Three must begin taking action independently . . ."

She pauses to look meaningfully at me.

". . . despite the discomfort this elicits."

She closes the manual.

What are you afraid of, Anna?

I am afraid of myself. Of spiraling out of control and falling into anorexia again. Of throwing away all the hard work I did this month because old habits die hard. Of leaving the treatment center at 6:00 P.M. and never coming back. I am afraid of dinner on my own.

I do not trust myself not to relapse.

She does not brush away my concern. I am grateful for that.

Instead, she says:

That may be the most honest sentence you have said to me since you came here.

I think of that. She may be right. To her and to myself. I decide to keep going, wobbly, down that line of thought.

This weekend was a one-time act I performed for my father. I cannot do this every day.

What other choice do you have?

Silence. None.

Do you want to stay here forever?

No!

Why not, Anna?

Because . . . Emm. Because I do not want to be Emm.

Or Julia. Or Valerie, but I do not tell the therapist that. Instead I say:

I am scared.

She nods. She is human again:

I know you are, Anna.

She changes tactics:

Let's say you weren't, why would you want to leave?

Because,

Because I want to buy my own cereal. Maybe even Lucky Charms. I want to go to the bathroom without asking for permission from anyone. I want to take a shower in the middle of the day. A long hot bath, actually. I want to go for a walk. Alone. I want to turn right instead of left.

Because I want to keep walking aimlessly till I discover a sidewalk café. I want to sit at a table outside and order sparkling wine at 4:00 P.M. I want to listen to someone play the guitar as I read and sip, soak sun and air, looking at the people passing by.

Because,

Because I also want to want something more than a walk and my choice of cereal. I want a goal. I want to make a list of goals. I want to have purpose again.

I was ambitious once. I was a dancer, a dreamer. I was loved, I was in love, I loved life. I once had books to read and places to see, babies I wanted to make. I want to want those again.

Because I think I want to live,

that life Katherine mentioned I may get. Hazy outlines of family Christmases; children; basil, mint, and thyme in clay pots.

I want more weekends like the one I just had,

more time with the people I love.

And what are those weekends worth?
Everything, I realize. Everything.
Worth eating?
Yes, worth eating.
Worth the weight and calories?
Yes.
And the pain and the anxiety at every meal?
Coffee and croissants, a conversation with Sophie. My father's famous omelettes. Crêpes on Sunday mornings with Matthias, stealing bites from his fork.
Yes,
because a birthday cake means a birthday celebration and ice cream means a good date. I can swallow the pain and anxiety if I can see that.

She looks at the clock; our time is almost up.

Let me summarize Stage Three: Patients continue treatment every day from eight to six. That will be at another facility. You will be assigned a new treatment team. You will take part in programming with another group of girls, and be responsible for your own dinner and evening snack.

Suddenly, I notice something. My head begins to spin.

I get to sleep at home. . . .
You get to sleep at home,
she says with a smile.

I get to sleep next to Matthias again.

88

Weight: 99 lbs.
BMI: 17

Summary:
Treatment team has approved patient transition to Stage Three of treatment, effective Monday, June 27, 2016. Patient will be transferred to the day treatment facility at 45 Forest Park Road.

Physiological Observations:
Patient weight has been increasing steadily and consistently with increases in meal plan. She remains significantly underweight but has been open to increasing food variety and reassessing body image distortions. No signs of refeeding syndrome. No other physical complications.

Psychological/Psychiatric Observations:
Patient has been completing meals and working on replacing negative eating-disorder behaviors with positive coping skills. She continues to struggle with poor body image but is working on challenging cognitive distortions.

Treatment Objectives:

Contingent upon medical stability and continued commitment to recovery, treatment team recommends a gradual and protracted increase in autonomy and exposure to normal life circumstances.

Patient will be required to present herself for treatment daily from 8:00 A.M. to 6:00 P.M. Patient will be allowed to complete dinner and evening snack alone and sleep at home.

Target caloric value: 3,500 calories daily, to be maintained upon discharge until adequate weight is reached.

89

My fifth and last Friday evening at 17 Swann Street. My last Friday-night date here with Matthias. It must be different.

I have an idea. I share it with Direct Care, who, to my surprise, says yes. She finds what I need easily enough: a box of colored chalk. Then, after lunch, she escorts me to the sunroom, where I spend twenty minutes on my knees, sketching and scribbling on the floor. I use up all the chalk.

At 7:26, I am long finished with dinner and peeking out the window. I am wearing my white dress for the occasion, pink lipstick, a little blush, my mother's pearl earrings, some perfume.

Matthias's blue car pulls into the driveway at 7:28. He does not know. I cannot wait to tell him, cannot wait for him to reach the front porch.

I open the door before he rings, too excited to wait.

Why, hello,

says a confused Matthias, taking in the dress.

You are being kidnapped,

he is informed before I put the blindfold on him.

In the dark, literally, Matthias is led through the house and into the sunroom.

And where am I going?

Away, with me.

He smiles.

I would love nothing more.

I guide Matthias to the perfect spot in the center of the room. Then I uncover his eyes and say:

You can look around now.

We are standing on a giant chalk drawing of a big jet plane, mostly white; it is purple in the spots where I ran out of chalk. Also more flying fish than plane. But he understands the idea and smiles: We are flying away.

My treatment team thinks that I am ready for Stage Three level of treatment.

Matthias makes no reaction at first. I emphasize:

Nonresidential treatment.

Slowly, very slowly, he asks:

Anna, what exactly does that mean?

That, if you don't mind, I would like to sleep at home on Monday night!

I cannot keep calm in any longer:

I still have to go to treatment every day, but I can leave after six! They say I am stable enough not to need night supervision!

Still no reaction.

I would have dinner and evening snack on my own. Well, ideally with you.

I smile.

I would sleep at home and come back the next day, like school.

I watch him cautiously process this:

No more visiting hours . . .

No, Matthias. No Direct Care watching us from the window. No more walks whose trajectory lines the borders of the garden around 17 Swann Street. No more sneaking around to kiss, no more saying goodbye, no more lonely bed.

I get my wife back,

he whispers, overwhelmed. Matthias finally understands.

This is not over,

I hasten to clarify.

It is just a phase transition.

He nods; we both understand that this is not the finish line. But we have come this far, haven't we? So far since that first day here. Keep walking.

Matthias takes me by the hand and we dance.

We dance, on a bad drawing of a big jet plane, in a sunroom at the back of a house with peach-pink walls at number 17, Swann Street. There is no music, but an entire orchestra is playing in our heads.

We had danced on the sidewalk on our first date, and months later, when we were married. I remember how close his face had been to mine, noticing every feature for the first time. I look

411

at them now: the freckle I had marked as my own under his right eye, his lashes that curved up. The scar on his upper lip, that had tasted of ice cream that first date, first kiss.

Since then we have danced in nightclubs and in bars, in kitchens and in hospital waiting rooms. Now, in a treatment center for women with eating disorders.

He is humming a song. I know the lyrics well:

. . . ride on a big jet plane.

Hey, hey . . .

He kisses me on the lips and says:

I will, you know.

What?

Take you away, in a big jet plane.

Where?

To Vienna, to Rome, to Phuket, Tokyo, and Havana. To the farthest place in the world from here. To wherever you want, but first, I was thinking, we could go home on Monday. And then to Paris.

Home, yes, and Paris, please. We dance on in the quiet room, to the end of visiting hours and a song no one else can hear. To violins, cello, and harp in a magnificent movement, and trilling, rippling piano keys. Then we step out of the plane and I walk Matthias back to the front door.

90

Monday morning. Six Mondays ago, my life was ending here. I open my eyes; it is still beautifully purple in the Van Gogh room. Vitals and weights soon, then the sun will rise, for the last time from this angle I hope. Then, after breakfast, I might as well carry my suitcase downstairs.

After the walk, I will have a few forms to sign, I suppose, then will spend the day with the girls, alternating meals, sessions, snacks. There may be new admissions, but they will be busy with orientation all day. I will not meet the patient who moves into this bedroom after me.

I get out of bed and wear my flower-print robe, flap to the front, for the last time. I head downstairs for vitals and weights early. Discharge Day has begun.

Two short hours later, the smell of coffee beckons me back down for breakfast. Yes, I would love a good cup of coffee now, and—

Surprise!

There are colorful streamers strewn across on the breakfast table. Glittering cards with my name on them. The girls are already at the table, each in her spot. I have a card for each of them too.

I hand them out, then sit down to this celebration of my Discharge Day, looking at every face, starting to feel emotional.

You girls are wonderful—

But Emm interrupts:

Coffee?

The pot of steaming black brew is passed around the table. No emotions, not yet. All right, Emm. At Direct Care's signal, we peel the plastic film off our bowls and reach for our spoons.

Monday is cereal day. My first bowl contains what looks like a whole tub of yogurt. In my second, a mountain, a mountain chain of sugar-coated, glistening cereal.

Frosties and vanilla yogurt. To think they had once paralyzed me. I sprinkle the light flakes onto the creamy swirls. There is silence around the table. Also, silence in my chest where, a few weeks ago, panic had been. I dip my spoon into the bowl and the earth remains still. I take a bite with academic curiosity.

Contrasts: smooth cream coating the hard, uneven ridges, little sugar crystals forming peaks. It feels cold and tastes cold. Hints of tangy and sweet. I listen to it crunch and crackle and wonder if one day it will be quiet in my head.

The patient manual clearly states:

Only 33% of women with anorexia nervosa

414

maintain full recovery after nine months. Of those, approximately one-third will relapse after the nine-month mark.

Next to me, Emm has not touched her yogurt yet.

No predictors of relapse exist.

Or of surviving treatment in the first place.

In the seat next to her, Sarah fills the silence by reading our horoscopes herself. We take them seriously, as the rules at 17 Swann Street say we should.

Full recovery of women with bulimia nervosa is significantly higher than anorexia,

I remember reading in the manual,

Up to 74% maintain recovery after the nine-month mark.

She then distributes copies of the daily word jumbles Emm brought. Silence again as we pore over them in between mushy and crunchy bites.

All eating disorders are chronic, and the risk of relapse remains. It is greatest within the four-to-nine-month period following discharge from inpatient care.

Tomorrow I will be eating breakfast at a different table, with different girls. Will I still be eating breakfast in four to nine months?

Symptoms may return.

Perhaps, but I have seven minutes of breakfast time left and a small hill of Frosties to swallow.

Then I have to run upstairs and zip my suitcase shut.

The minute hand on the clock hits eight thirty. My last breakfast is over. The dirty dishes are piled high in the sink, and we are dismissed.

In community space, the discussion of the day is about what I will do when I leave. Will I go back to my old job at the supermarket? I hope not. Will I go back to school? Will I try to have a baby? Will I start dancing again?

I do not know,

I reply. And I genuinely do not. One step, one day, one meal at a time.

What would all of you do?

Dreams fly around the room like the streamers that had colored the breakfast table. Travel plans, family plans, career, love, life goals. Emm remains silent. She speaks last.

Her dream overrules all of ours:

If I could leave, I would go on a walk. A very long walk in the countryside. Somewhere fresh, with my sister. Maybe talk, but mostly just walk, I think.

I know Emm would not appreciate me reaching for her hand in public. No superfluous words or display of emotion; our friendship was not built that way.

Direct Care comes in.

Morning walk, ladies?

Emm, of course, leads the way.

By the time we return I have gathered enough courage to go to her. She is in her alcove. The daily jumbles, and my card I see, are in her hand.

I think I like your suggestion best.

She looks at me, confused.

About what I should do when I leave here. I'd like a walk in the countryside, and

I pause,

I would like you to come too.

I notice the change in her expression; I am crossing a line, I know. I keep going:

I want you to leave 17 Swann Street and go on a walk with me. I know I am not your sister, and I know you do not want to. But I also know you can and that there are Olympics every four years.

Pause for breath and courage.

We do not have to talk. We can just walk and breathe, but I need you to walk and breathe with me. I'll wait as long as you need me to.

Why?

I shrug. *Because that is what we do, Emm.*

At six fifteen, I do not say goodbye to the girls. I cannot. In fact, as they line up for dinner, the last thing I tell them is a lie: I forgot to empty my cubby.

Do not wait for me. I will do that then follow you.

Direct Care does not contradict me. She and I

watch them walk away, across the grass and into the house adjacent to 17 Swann Street.

I was a part of that picture for so long. How strange it feels to stand here. I am not cured. I am not ready; I am terrified of what is coming. But I lift my chin higher. *Keep walking, Anna.* I see Matthias's blue car drive down the street.

My blue suitcase. One last walk through the house at 17 Swann Street. Its peach-pink walls, the orange-pink sky, the pink magnolia tree. Goodbye to Direct Care, then we leave her and all of this behind us, radio off, windows rolled down, my hand on Matthias's shifting gears.

The car turns at the end of the street, and the house disappears. I am going home. We are going home. I get to sleep next to Matthias tonight.

91

The carols are playing on loop in my head, but I do not mind. It is nearly Christmas in a year I did not think would end. It is nearly Christmas and snowing outside, and for once it looks beautiful. It is nearly 7:00 P.M. Matthias's stomach is grumbling on the couch.

He is half naked, half asleep. My eyes trace the contour of his chest. I know every crevice, every ridge, every freckle by heart. I spent the last six months rediscovering them. Rediscovering me and how my head fit under his chin, my ear over his heart. I can see it, just barely, pulsing from where I sit.

Six months since I last slept alone in Patient Bedroom Number 5 of a peach-pink house on 17 Swann Street. I have not been back. I am far from cured; it has been long and difficult. 8:00 A.M. to 6:00 P.M., every day. But every night I have had dinner with Matthias and fallen asleep next to him.

Dinner tonight will be quick and easy: spaghetti with tomatoes, basil, and rosemary, fresh from the pots on the windowsill. Matthias will chop some salad on the side, and there should be some Chianti left. Tufts of snow are floating delicately down Furstenberg Street. I wonder if it is snowing on Swann Street as well.

I think of that house and those girls every day. At 9:10, the morning walk. My heart breaks at morning rain, because it means they must stay indoors. At twelve thirty they sit down to lunch. I sit down to lunch too. I am scared with them and breathe with relief when, at one fifteen, it is done. Then they have apple cinnamon tea. I have ginger sometimes. I think of them most of all at dusk. I miss them terribly.

I did not choose anorexia. I did not choose to starve. But every morning, over and over, I choose to fight it, again.

The spaghetti is ready.

Matthias.

He stirs but his eyelids remain subbornly shut in protest. I go to the couch, kiss each, then his nose. Then his cheeks. And get carried away. Within seconds he is wide awake, fighting me off, kissing me, laughing.

When he finally lets me come up for breath to announce,

Dinner is ready,

the boy I love kisses the girl he married and says:

Dinner can wait.

My name is Anna, and I am the luckiest girl in the world. I am a dancer, a constant daydreamer.

I like sparkling wine in the late afternoon, ripe and juicy strawberries in June. Quiet mornings make me happy, dusk makes me blue. Like Whistler, I like gray and foggy cities. I see purple in gray and foggy days. I believe in the rich taste of real vanilla ice cream, melting stickily from a cone.

I believe in love. I am still madly in love, I am still madly loved. I have books to read, places to see, babies to make, birthday cakes to taste. I even have unused birthday wishes to spare.

But now the spaghetti is cold and we are running late.

We sit down to eat. Matthias announces that it tastes good anyway, and that I have sauce on my chin. I laugh through my last slurpy bite. He has seconds.

We do the dishes clumsily. Orchid watered, lights out. Suitcases zipped, we dash out the door. We have a plane to catch. To Paris. *Hey, hey.*

Acknowledgments

Thank you,

Mon chéri, for not letting me quit;

Merya, for not letting me quit;

Mamy, Papi, and Marwan, for not letting me quit;

Scott, for not letting me quit;

Amy Tannenbaum, for not letting me quit;

Claudia, Maggie, Colette, and Joe, for not letting me quit.

Thank you, Paul and Corky, Andrej and Jessica, Anne, Cooper, and Tika, for visiting 17 Swann Street.

Thank you, Leslie Gelbman, for falling in love with 17 Swann Street.

Thank you, Alienor Moore, Henri Mohrman, Riwa Zwein, Lynn Dagher, Helen and Karen Karam, Jane Swim, Isabelle Hoët, Rose McInerney, Jen Enderlin, Dori Weintraub, Tiffany Shelton, and everyone at St. Martin's Press, and most importantly,

thank you to the girls at 17 Swann Street.

Yara

Author's Note

17 Swann Street is a fictional place, but eating disorders are very real. Anorexia nervosa, bulimia nervosa, binge eating, and others, are mental illnesses, not poor habits, and those who have them are suffering greatly. These diseases are quiet and deadly.

They do not have to be.

Anna is the luckiest girl in the world; she has anorexia, but she is alive. She is recovering because she has access to treatment and support from those who love her. Not everyone does, but everyone should. So if, while reading this story, you recognize bits of your own self or someone you love, please say something.

Contact a therapist or doctor. Call an eating disorder hotline. Help is available online and via text as well if you prefer. Talk to that someone you love. Talk to that someone who loves you.

Please say something. I know it is difficult. The conversation that follows will be too, but it could alter the story before it ends at 17 Swann Street.

I hope this helps.

I wish you well,

Yara

Center Point Large Print
600 Brooks Road / PO Box 1
Thorndike, ME 04986-0001 USA

(207) 568-3717

US & Canada:
1 800 929-9108
www.centerpointlargeprint.com